20/

Carol Drinkwater

MOLLY

GW00976386

MACDONALD YOUNG BOOKS

One

My mum used to say that we shouldn't have a dog because we live in a flat. Then a few years ago, Dad bought me a puppy for my ninth birthday. A golden retriever. I called her Red. She was great. Red – not because we're communists, but Red like the women with flaming hair in gangster films.

Mum was pretty mad at Dad for buying the dog. When they thought I wasn't listening they had a real old tiff about it. But after a couple of days Mum accepted Red. In fact she loved her as much as I did. Things were brilliant for a while.

I used to get home from school, all set to take Red to the park, and find Dad playing the trumpet to her in the kitchen. Red'd be leaping about, barking. Dad said he was teaching her to sing and that when she was good enough they'd go on the telly and do an act on one of those daft shows like Become a Star, *or whatever they're called. We knew he was kidding, of course.*

He's a professional musician. Really brilliant jazz, he plays, and in those days he was doing well and had plenty of work.

Anyway, Dad used to dress Red in Mum's apron or a tea towel or whatever was to hand and then he'd do an impersonation of being on the show. He'd act all daft and tongue-tied introducing himself and Red, about to do their spot. Mum and me would fall about laughing. Red just kept barking, getting excited and puzzled, which made us laugh all the more.

Then one day Red got out. None of us ever found out how. She ran into the street and got killed. It was horrible. I cried for days, so did Mum. We all did. Mum blamed Dad. She said he should never have bought Red in the first place. But that was unfair. And though he said nothing I could see Dad was pretty cut up.

It was round about then that everything started going wrong. Dad stopped having plenty of work. He got moody, said things like: "This country's got a lot to answer for."

Then he started staying out — sometimes all night, sometimes for more than one night.

I'd catch Mum crying. When I asked what was up, she just smiled — one of those inane adult smiles that are meant to fool you but don't. She said I was imagining things; that Dad was working.

Now Dad says he wants to leave England and go and live in Paris. He says this country's had it — maybe it has. How do I know? But if he wants us all to leave, that's OK with me. Sure I'd miss my friends, but I hate to see him moping about with nothing to do and not coming home, and Mum with red eyes all the time. Red, yeah, red. I don't care where we live.

I just want us to be happy like we used to be.

Mum thinks I can't see she's crying.

They think I haven't sussed something's up…

Molly Greenfield read over what she had written. She underlined the last sentence savagely and then tossed biro and notebook to the floor. They settled amongst a clutch of rented videos, chocolate wrappers, sneakers and the everyday jumble which lay mounting alongside her unmade bed. She stared out of the window at the dingy brick wall of the neighbouring block of flats. From the busy street beneath rose the honking of rush-hour traffic.

Today was Friday — a Friday in the middle of August.

Another warm, sunny day in the long procession of days that made up her summer holidays.

After breakfast Molly was going rollerskating on Primrose Hill with a bunch of pals from her comprehensive school. Later, after a Coke at the greasy spoon café in Regent's Park, she'd stroll up to Swiss Cottage to the Odeon cinema.

Molly thought that going to the pictures was the neatest way of spending her afternoons. Nothing in the world to beat it. Whenever she had money to spare (not often) and time to kill (plenty) the cinema was where she'd go.

Alone in the darkness, usually without cash left over to buy popcorn, Molly gave herself up, transported by the magic the cinema conjured up for her.

Molly dreamed of making her own films. That was why she was always writing, scribbling down ideas and thoughts, pouring it all out into scruffy notebooks.

Writing also helped when she was feeling mixed-up, or blue, like now. She wanted to feel good, but she was troubled. She hadn't slept for two nights. It had been too hot. She hadn't been eavesdropping, but she had heard things.

The living room was next to her room. Even when her parents turned up the telly or spoke in whispers, she could hear.

She could pick out the rows.

It was the tone, the speed with which they answered one another – *tecktecktecK*! – like a constant crossfire of bullets in a Western. She could never make out the words, but she knew they were saying stuff which dug at one another.

Life was pretty dicey at the moment. The atmosphere was horrible. Take the day before, for instance.

The day before, her mum, Alice Greenfield, had worn her dressing gown at breakfast. That in itself was alarming; usually she was dressed before anyone. Then Molly had noticed her mum's eyes. They had been puffy while her nose was red and sore-looking, and she had been sniffing – sniffing continuously while picking like a bird at a bowl of muesli. She didn't have a cold. *She had been trying her best not to cry.*

When Alice wasn't upset, she'd say stuff like, "Molly, you're eating too quickly", "Careful not to spill the milk, dear," or "Have you combed your hair?"

Yesterday morning she'd barely opened her mouth.

Then Molly's dad had appeared, arriving home after a night out at the clubs. As usual he'd been carrying his trumpet, but he hadn't looked as though he'd come from a really neat music session. He'd looked bedraggled and edgy, like "Just-don't-say-anything. I'm-not-in-the-mood, OK?"

No one had spoken. There'd been a really heavy silence. You could hear the teaspoons stirring and landing, *clunk*! against the saucers. They couldn't have sounded louder if they'd been recorded on stereo.

Molly had felt helpless. She'd chewed the same mouthful of cereal over and over because she'd been too knotted up to swallow it. It couldn't have tasted worse if she'd eaten the packet. All the while she'd been racking her brains for something to say – "*Look, I'm not dumb. I live here too. Why don't you tell me what you're rowing about?*" – but she'd lacked the courage.

She'd decided to skip it and just say that, if it was OK with everyone, she'd go to the pictures later.

Then, *at that very instant*, as she'd opened her mouth to speak, her father had turned to her and, with a broad grin and a wink, had said, "I bet you'd kill to see a film today, eh, Moll?" And he'd handed her a *five-pound note!*

No kidding! Just dug into his big, baggy shirt and passed it across the cornflakes packet without her even asking for it! "Gee, thanks, Dad." Quick as lightning, before her mother'd objected, she'd slipped it into her pocket.

But Molly hadn't gone to the cinema.

Back in her bedroom, stuffing swimming things into a carrier bag, she'd felt a creeping sense of lousiness.

Could she really disappear for the entire day when her mum was so upset? She couldn't.

So, while Alice was doing the housework, she'd nipped to the outdoor pool and taken a dip. Then she'd come home and together they'd ridden the bus to Oxford Street, shopping.

Molly hadn't mentioned the rows. She'd wanted to, but she hadn't, even though she sensed that her mum had understood why she'd gone shopping with her. Molly hated shopping.

So, that was yesterday. Today, Molly *definitely* intended to spend her dad's fiver at the cinema.

No reason to feel selfish today; it was Friday and her mum went to Sainsbury's on Fridays. She'd be fine. She met other mums. They drank coffee and commiserated about the shocking cost of things.

Molly *hated* supermarkets even more than regular up-and-down-the-same-street type of shopping, especially that huge Sainsburys behind the lost-its-franchise, breakfast-telly station near where they lived in Camden Town. Going to the movies would cheer her up, stop her fretting about her folks.

She slipped off the bed and hurried down the hall towards the kitchen. Along the way she popped her head round the door of her parents' room. The bed was made, unlike hers, and the room was silent except for the clock ticking.

There was no sign of her dad. She hadn't heard him at all this morning. He must have stayed out again.

Molly's heart felt leaden as she pushed open the kitchen door, but she grinned brightly. "Morning!"

"You haven't combed your hair." (Her mother's greeting.) It was better than silence.

"I'm going to the park, skating."

"That doesn't stop you combing your hair."

Molly thought it was wild the way her mum always fussed about her hair but never commented when her socks were odd or her shirt was runkled because she'd filched clothes from the laundry basket before Alice had ironed them. Even at night, when Molly was climbing into bed, her mum always asked her if she'd combed her hair!

Molly had wild blonde hair which grew like drinking straws. In cartoons when one of the characters gets a fright, their hair stands up. That was Molly's permanent style – Vertical Chic! The colour was pretty strange too. Everyone thought it was bleached, but it wasn't.

As Molly lifted the cornflakes packet she noticed an envelope in her cereal bowl. "What's this?"

"Good news."

"Where's Dad?" *Very casual*, Molly's tone.

"He went out early."

Not true.

Molly shot her mum a glance. Alice's head was lowered, her eyes averted; she was studying a bill.

Molly let it go. She poured the cornflakes with her left hand while pulling the letter out of the envelope with the right and her teeth.

"WOW! IT *IS* GOOD NEWS!"

She hurled both letter and cornflakes into the air. "Whooey!" she yipped. They fell like snow all around her.

Alice began laughing. "I'm so proud of you. You clever girl!"

"What did Dad say?"

"He left before the post," her mother lied.

Outside, the sun beat down. Weaving her way in and out of the traffic, Molly charged through the streets of north London towards Primrose Hill. Her skates bumped against her as she darted happily across the roads.

Nearby, from one of the exits of Camden Town tube station, her father surfaced. He spotted his dishevelled tomboy, Molly, in her leopard-skin leggings and oversized boots and called out to her, but she didn't hear him.

Molly was dashing to reach Primrose Hill, to find Jenny, her best friend and tell her the brilliant news.

Molly and Jenny, with three other pals, were sprawled on the Primrose Hill grass.

"A private college in France!" repeated Jenny for the umpteenth time. "What did your mum and dad say?"

Eyes closed, like napping cats, flushed from exertion, they were basking in the sunshine after several frenetic hours of rollerskating. In the distance, beyond the meshed aviaries of Regent's Park Zoo, the Post Office Tower was visible. A portable radio tuned to Capital 195 was playing Bruce Springsteen. A selection of emptied drink cans lay scattered amongst the rich green leaves of the dandelions.

"Mum's dead pleased. Dad doesn't know yet." Swiftly, before Jenny could ask why, Molly added, "He was up and out before the post."

Jenny made no response. She was remembering the things her parents said about Molly's mum and dad and she was considering how Molly's news was going to affect *her*. She was about to lose her best friend.

Molly stared up at the bright blue sky, contemplating its hugeness. This very same sky looked down over France as well. She rolled across the daisy heads and prodded her dozing pal. "Let's go! I'm ravenous."

"Where to?" Jenny's eyes remained closed.

"Back to my place."

"Can't today."

"Why not?"

"I have to be home early."

Molly knew this wasn't true. She raised herself up on her elbows. Eyes alert and querying, she studied Jenny's expression, considering the lie. "It's Friday; your mum's working. You don't have to be home till six."

Jenny curled up like a sleeping squirrel, her face hidden from Molly's.

"What are you two whispering about?" Josephine, a lanky-haired brunette and owner of the transistor radio, stood up. She kicked the sole of Molly's left boot with the toe of her slingback. "You going to the cinema later, Molly?"

"You bet."

"I'll see you there then, three-thirty."

"You're on."

"I'm going for a pizza. Anyone coming?" shouted Josephine, already descending the hill, waving. "See you, guys!" Seconds later, clobber gathered together, Isabelle and Sandra departed, leaving Molly and Jenny alone.

"Jen?"

Jenny opened her eyes. Molly's face was beaming in on her. It made Jenny feel squirmy – those great green eyes lasering into her brain, reading her thoughts. She often felt that about Molly, even though she was her best friend. It was as though Molly was burrowing about inside her brain. Jenny reached into her pocket for the red plastic sunglasses she had bought that morning from a stallholder in Camden Market. She slipped them on.

"Cool shades," observed Molly.

"Nothing's up, if that's what you're thinking."

"Yes, there is."

"Stop staring! You ask too many questions. Even my mum says so!"

This last remark quite took Molly by surprise. On a less auspicious day it might have hurt her. "I only wanted to know if you're coming back to my place or not."

Jenny rose hastily and brushed the earth from her shorts. "I can't stay long," she replied testily, lifting her skates from the grass and scrambling off down the hill, leaving Molly, bewildered, to hurry on after her.

They walked in silence along littered streets. It was Jenny who spoke first.

"I can't imagine it. Leaving my best friend, moving to another country…"

"We'll stay in touch. You can come and visit me. And I'll visit my mum and dad every weekend in Paris."

"Not even living with your parents! But I guess it's different for you, you've got no brothers and sisters… and…"

The hesitancy in Jenny's voice alerted Molly who stopped dead right there in the high street outside Marks and Spencer. She stared at her friend, knowing that something she wouldn't want to hear was coming. An old lady wheeling a shopping trolley full of greens and biscuits accidently bashed Jenny in the back, knocking her closer to Molly.

"And what, Jen?"

Jenny's mouth went dry. She gave up on her sentence.

"And what, Jen?"

Why did Molly always persist? It was like being best friends with a policeman!

Jenny walked on, but Molly drew her back. Those big green eyes stared hard, looking concerned and determined.

Jenny wished she hadn't begun, but she had and now she was cornered. "My mum… thinks it's for the best."

"What is?"

"Your scholarship. She thinks it'd be good for you. To get away—"

"Get away from what?"

"Your parents."

Molly gazed incredulously at her friend. "It's none of your mum's bloody business!"

"I'm going." Jenny stormed off, disappearing amongst a flurry of afternoon shoppers.

"Jen! Jenny! Wait! Don't go, please!"

Jenny didn't look back.

Molly caught up with her outside Waterstone's bookshop, where Jenny was peering in the window. Thank heavens, thought Molly, for her friend's addiction to books.

"Don't be mad, Jen. I'm sorry."

The two girls made a detour back along the high street to pick up a couple of chocolate chip ice creams. By the time they reached Molly's block of flats all tension between them had evaporated. They were giggling together about "yukky Roger Tanret", a carrot-haired boy they'd bumped into at the ice cream parlour. He had a mad crush on Molly – or so Jenny reckoned, but

Molly thought that was stupid.

"Roger Tanret loves Molly Greenfield!" shrieked Jenny at the top of her voice. The words rang out and spiralled back down the stairwell. "And Molly Green—"

"Shut up!" squealed Molly. "The whole building'll hear you."

They climbed the stone stairs, hollering and whooping, spirits high. Molly turned her key and shoved open the door.

In the kitchen, straight ahead of them, stood Molly's parents. Her dad was gripping her mum by the shoulders. At first Molly thought they were embracing. Then she realized they were having a fight, both shouting, something about money. Neither of them had heard the girls come in.

Molly stood in the doorway, watching. Jenny held back, a pace or two behind. Molly's dad raised his hand above his head. He seemed all set to land it on her mum! *Violent*, that's how it looked to Molly! But that couldn't be what it was. Probably her dad was gesticulating like that because he was mad as hell.

But before Molly could get to grips with what was really going on, she panicked and started yelling. "Dad! Don't! Don't!" The words just came whooshing out of her stupid mouth.

Jenny must have read the situation the same way or maybe it was Molly's cry that freaked her – whichever. When Molly screamed Jenny ditched her ice cream and took off, descending the stairs at a pace as though nothing mattered except getting out of there. The *clomp! clomp!* of her platforms echoed as she went.

Molly was shivering. Her legs had turned to jelly.

She'd misread it. For sure she had. *Her dad would never in a million years hit her mum.*

Both her parents were staring at her. She stared back

at them helplessly. Then she thought about Jenny and Jenny's mum, and the others, and what all their mums were going to say when the gossip got about. She swung back and leaned out over the banisters, calling her friend's name. Jenny's fleeing figure kept on moving until it disappeared beyond the stairwell.

Molly had to stop her – stop Jen blabbing to everyone about what she'd seen! Without another thought she took flight, hurling herself down the stairs two, three steps at a time. But by the time she reached the entrance Jenny was nowhere to be seen.

Molly hid in her room, buried under the duvet, curtains closed, door locked. Hidden in the darkness, she wanted nothing but to be left alone. She wanted to die.

The next morning she crawled out of bed and went in search of her dad in his room. He wasn't there. Nor was his trumpet on the shelf in the wardrobe where he kept it, and on the side where he always hung his clothes, there was an empty space.

Molly stood alone in the middle of her parents' room and wept.

She didn't hear her mum come in. It was only when Alice spoke that she realized someone else was there.

"What's going on?" Molly asked.

Alice crossed the soft carpet, arms outstretched, and led Molly to the bed. They sat side by side. Molly could tell by her mum's pale face that the news wasn't terrific.

"Your father's… left."

"Left?" Molly pulled away. Stunned, lips numb and prickly as if someone had hit her, she rose, took a deep breath and began to pace up and down. She couldn't stay still. Anyway, she didn't want to be so close to her mother. However illogical, she felt angry towards her, as though all this was Alice's fault, even if she somehow understood that it couldn't be.

"What about our plans? I thought we were moving to Paris. Dad said he'd find work in a jazz club—"

"We'll still go."

"Without Dad?"

"He'll visit us."

"But he's not going to live with us any more?"

"Not right now, no."

Terror shot through Molly like a firework. "But why? Don't you love each other any more?" She thought of how proud she'd felt when she'd learned about her scholarship to the private college in France – her contribution to their new beginning, to her dad's chances of finding work in Paris. It was why she'd swotted so hard, why she'd wanted to go there in the first place. "What about me?"

"In a few weeks you'll be off to your new school—"

"I'm not going!"

"Of course you are."

"I'm staying here!"

Her mother rose from the bed and drew Molly towards her. "We're both very proud of you."

Molly shrugged her away. "Dad didn't even mention it."

She turned and hurried from the room.

He really had left home.

They didn't hear a word from him. It was as though he'd disappeared off the face of the earth. When Molly went enquiring at all his favourite haunts, nobody had seen him. She felt desperate. Every time the phone rang she tore along the hallway to get to it first, praying it would be him. Every film she saw – and she went to see plenty because it was the only place she could escape her misery – she wanted to share with him, to describe the scenes she'd liked best, the way she'd always done. The way he'd encouraged her to.

She wrote him letters which she screwed up and threw on the floor. She had no address for them. Her room began to look like the centre court at Wimbledon! When she asked Alice if he was in Paris, her mum replied, "I don't know dear." It made Molly mad at her. Madder than she already was.

They went shopping. Hours spent waiting for buses in Oxford Street. Up and down escalators, in and out of stores searching for stuff for her new school. Whatever she liked her mother judged unsuitable. What kind of a place was this college, anyway? Molly sulked, Alice told her she was being a pain, and once again they argued.

September came. The holidays were drawing to a close. Molly's pals were preparing for their return to school. She listened to their chatter. The same topics, but now she had no part in them. She had become an outsider.

Even Jenny was cooler towards her. She'd grown aloof and disinterested, not like a best friend. Molly invited her back to her place and Jenny refused. When Molly asked why, Jenny said she'd been forbidden to go.

"Why?"

"My parents were freaked about the violence."

"No, you're wrong. It wasn't violence. That wasn't how it was," said Molly, but she was mortified.

Her mum packed boxes, called estate agents in Paris, crossed stuff off lists and pestered Molly to get her room packed up.

Whenever Molly tried to talk, Alice seemed preoccupied. She was "brushing up" on her French, "going back over the basics."

This involved repeating daft phrases back at a cassette in the kitchen.

"Tournez à gauche au bureau de poste."
"Tourner à gauche au bureau de poste?"
"Oui, tournez à gauche au bureau de poste."
"Ah, tourner à gauche au bureau de poste!"

And still there was no news from her dad. It was as though he didn't exist any more and no one except Molly held fast to the memory of their lives together. The music had gone – all that terrific jazz. And the armchair in the living room where he used to sit and polish his trumpet was now occupied by a tea crate full of straw and china.

Everything was changing and the only person who could do nothing about it was Molly.

Two

Paris was the city Molly's dad loved best. He often talked about the life he had lived there when he was young. It was where her parents had first met.

When Molly and her mum arrived, it was drizzling. They wove their way through the narrow streets, negotiating a never-ceasing jumble of traffic, searching out the signs which led them to *Paris Centre*. All the drivers were honking their horns, as though they were riding bumper cars at the fair. Alice was heroic. She hooted right back and motored on. Molly was impressed.

The flat her mum had rented for them was in Belleville, a down-at-heel district of Paris. Molly loved it at first sight. It was energetic, shabby, foreign and unconventional; there were cafés all over the place with hip-looking people sitting about and waiters buzzing to and fro carrying trays laden with drinks. There were cinemas showing films from African countries she'd barely heard of, youngsters dancing on the pavements, musicians crouched in doorways playing the blues.

Paris was brilliant, attitude: cool, with its alien aromas of coffee and tobacco.

One of the exterior walls of their block had been covered with graffiti-pictures, as well as slogans. It reminded Molly of a photo she'd seen in one of the

Sunday magazines of a man whose whole body was a mass of tattoos.

The flat was empty when they got there. Even their beds hadn't arrived. That night they slept on their clothes, laid out in piles on the floor. It wasn't like real life at all – it was brilliant.

"I can see why Dad likes it here," she said to her mother the following morning. They were climbing the steep hill back to their block. At every step Molly scanned the streets, willing her father to appear from out of nowhere, hoping that on any corner or in the doorway of one of the many out-of-the-way jazz clubs she might spot him. "Do you think he's here somewhere?"

Alice shrugged. "I don't know where he is."

"Don't you care?"

"Of course."

This response, and her mother's silence on the subject, puzzled and concerned Molly.

Although she loved this new city – the parts she had visited, at least – it troubled her that they'd made this move without him. He might never find them again.

She worried that one morning he'd stroll up to the door of their flat in London, humming a tune, swinging his trumpet case the way he always did, slip his key in the lock and discover new people, another family, living there. *In their home*. How would he take it when he learnt that she and her mum had left the country?

He might simply give up on them, shrug them out of his life, like an old coat.

Molly had written out their new address on dozens of bits of paper torn from notebooks. These she'd deposited with everybody she could think of: friends, relatives, stallholders at the market, shopkeepers... Hand-scribbled notes awaited Peter Greenfield all over

London, for the day when he came looking for her. She was sure that day would come.

Molly even began to wonder whether her mum had gone barmy. Moving home, changing countries for no real reason... Perhaps, like in books, she was sick with love for Peter, had lost her mind and returned to the city where they'd met.

Molly felt impelled to broach the subject, to try to come to grips with what was going on inside her mum's head.

They visited the Eiffel Tower. There were musicians playing at the foot of the tower, there were artists sketching portraits for passers-by, there were fruit stalls, hot-dog stands, even a clown walking on his hands. She hoped her dad might be there, busking, but there was no sign of him.

"I'm not clear about why we've moved here... to France." They stared out across the misty city spread like fingers beneath them. "I mean, why am I being sent away to this college?"

Alice laughed and touched her daughter softly on the cheek. "It was you who worked so hard to win the scholarship."

"Yeah, but that was before Dad left, when I wanted to make you both proud of me, when we were all going to live here in Paris together. A new beginning, Dad said. I don't see the point now."

"Let's give it a try, shall we?"

"But why?"

"There's no work in England. Your father's had a very difficult time. He's a good musician; he deserves a chance. Once he's settled in Paris and found himself a job everything will look brighter. And then we'll be waiting for him. His family. That's why I want you to go to the college."

"But he won't know where to find us."

"He will."

"If he comes while I'm away you'll tell him where I am, won't you?"

"What a silly thing. Of course I will."

"You want him to come back, don't you?"

But her mother refused to discuss it further. Instead she drew her daughter's attention to the approaching evening, settling like dust over the lovely city that was now their home. "Time to go, sweetheart," she whispered.

The following day Alice delivered Molly to her new school in the mountains – the Trouvai International College.

Side by side they gazed about them at the buildings and the alpine countryside. Molly's backpack, hanging from between her fingers, scuffed the ground. She scratched at it with the toe of her boot.

It would have been difficult to find a more remote location. In every direction tall spruce trees shot like candles from endless mountains. Her eyes roamed to the left. In a flat parkland she sighted four tennis courts. They were deserted, no doubt because the term was yet to begin. On a second glance she observed there wasn't a soul to be seen in *any* direction. The entire place gave off an uninhabited air.

"It's very tranquil, dear," Alice reassured.

It was so dead you could hear the cones growing! Beyond the buildings lay a vast woodland, oak and more spruce, intended, no doubt, for brisk fresh-air walks and nature studies. Ugh!

A painted arrow pointed the direction to the students' dormitories. Another, to the administration block.

Molly's heart sank into her new boots. She thought of

the city, of all the films she wouldn't be seeing, of all her pals enjoying themselves back in England. All at once, even her mental picture of carrot-haired Roger Tanret, her admirer, had grown appealing! Then she remembered a film in which the young heroine was dying of some unknown disease and some well-meaning relative packed her off to the mountains in Switzerland to recuperate. This could be the location! That was it! This whole exercise was a set-up! She had contracted some horrible terminal disease and her parents couldn't bring themselves to break it to her!

Jeez! She almost wished it were true. At least her days here would be numbered!

Molly let out a long, low groan. "It looks like a hospital."

A sudden wind whipped at their faces and the gravel crackled like popcorn under their feet as they made their way across the track towards a dreary-looking, red-brick wing. This housed the administration offices.

And then the most unlikely thing occurred.

Within the admin block, leaning against a glass partition, stood a man. At first sight only the silhouette of his back was visible, then he turned his head and she recognized his profile.

"It's Dad!" Molly whooped.

It was definitely him. She knew it without a shadow of a doubt. "It is!" She took off at a gallop, shouting, "Dad, Dad!" and charging through the swing doors to greet him.

There he was, by the receptionist's window, with a broad smile on his face. His manner was so casual that it might have been a matter of hours since they'd last seen one another.

"I was beginning to think you weren't coming," was all he said, laughing as he spoke. He was looking tired, but definitely pleased to see her. Molly hurled herself into his open arms, clutching his jacket and hugging him tightly. Six long weeks of love and missing.

"Where have you been? Why haven't you called us?" she whispered in his ear, trying not to care that the receptionist was typing within earshot and could no doubt hear every word.

"Oh… I'm in Paris, trying to sort out a job."

"So are we! Where? Where are you?"

At that moment Alice approached. Molly couldn't ignore the look her parents exchanged, the tension and the discomfort in their faces. It hurt her to see the two people she loved most in the whole world behaving clumsily in one another's presence, when once upon a time they had been so carefree.

"We're living there, too, aren't we, Mum? Mum found us a brilliant new flat. It's in Belleville. You could drive back with her, couldn't he, Mum?"

The director of the college was Madame Savère, a tall, thin woman with a face like a greyhound.

Madame *Severe*, thought Molly, staring across the desk at those icy, piercing eyes enlarged by tortoiseshell specs.

"I am delighted to be given this opportunity of meeting you both, particularly because I know how very busy you are, Mr Greenfield."

Molly shot a glance at her father, seated to her left. His hands rested in his lap, fingers bunched together like bananas.

He coughed self-consciously before replying. If she hadn't known that within the hour her parents would be abandoning her she might have found the situation amusing. "Yes… I was anxious to be here…"

She knew her dad hated any sort of formal interview.

That was what made his being there all the more special. He'd even dug out a suit! Good old Dad!

Peter's words disintegrated into silence.

Madame Savère picked up the thread and ploughed on. "I am confident, Molly, that you will be very happy here."

Not a chance, thought Molly despondently.

"Your tests were particularly strong in composition and essay writing…"

Still Molly said nothing. Was a response expected of her? Best to keep quiet.

"Your daughter has a very fertile imagination…" Madame Savère was addressing her parents now.

"Our young Molly's heart is in the cinema," Peter explained.

Madame Savère creased her pointed face and stared determinedly at a form on the desk in front of her. "Yes, I noted that. Unfortunately we have nothing so specialized here, but we do have a splendid summer course in drama. Perhaps you will stay on during your holidays and participate in that."

Stay on for the holidays!

Still clutching her backpack, Molly was led away to the registrar's corner where a form containing a complex list of questions was handed to her. Each question was written in *four* languages.

"Fill this out, please," a voice requested.

From where she was leaning Molly threw furtive glances back towards her parents. They were deep in *sotto voce* conversation with Madame Savère.

Actually, the headmistress was doing all the talking. Molly's dad wasn't saying anything much at all. He was simply staring at his shoes while her mum, brow furrowed, listened intently, nodding a great deal.

Molly sighed.

*

"You'll do all right here, Moll," her father muttered when they were standing outside by Alice's car.

Molly *knew*, by all that self-conscious coughing, that he was feeling as helpless about all of this as she was. She stared directly into his face, one of those big-eyed, pleading stares that usually worked. She wanted him to hijack her, take her away from all this, fly her somewhere on the notes of a magic trumpet. To a land rich in music and films!

Not this time, Moll. No such luck.

After one more hug from each of her parents she watched as they got into the car. Her lip began to quiver. Shoot! Whatever happened she mustn't break down. Not here, not now. She held up her hand and waved cheerily, biting hard against the inside of her cheek.

"Dad?" she called at the last moment, surprising even herself.

"Yes?"

"Promise you'll write."

Her mother started up their old motor. Molly's voice quavered. Lucky for her, the tremor had been hidden by the engine turning over and rattling like old bones.

"Soon as I'm settled." He gave her a wink. Within minutes her parents were speeding along the winding driveway and Molly was left standing alone, her gaze blurred by salty tears.

Three

The first weeks of college, those early grappling weeks, were tough going. Molly failed to make a bond with any of the girls in her dormitory. The truth was, she was miserable – missing Paris, pining to be there, longing to be with her family. She dreamt of discovering her dad's favourite city alongside him, checking out the clubs with him; and she dreamt of getting her folks firmly back on the road to reconciliation. Her mum and dad together again – that was Molly's objective.

But how could she achieve that from Trouvai, stuck up in the mountains at college? She felt about as useful as a relief parcel in no man's land.

Molly had been assigned to Dormitory Seven, which she shared with four other girls: Daniela Lubicz, the softest (least terrifying) of the bunch, Nathalie, Angela and Vanessa Goldstein. All of the girls were Molly's age except Vanessa, who was fifteen. Vanessa was something else! Like a fast-talking chick out of a Martin Scorsese movie, she was an amazing looking, spoilt, confident New York American and most definitely the leader of the pack. Which was fine by Molly. She had no designs on the rôle. In fact, Molly had no designs on any rôle at college; she had only one idea in her head – plotting her escape.

Down a drainpipe in the dead of night, across the grass, through the pine forest, beating a nifty retreat. Purchasing a beret as disguise (*à la* French Resistance), a lone figure trekking north through the French countryside. Or buried beneath mounds of dirty linen (ugh!) in the laundry basket, or strapped to the belly of a lorry, choking from the fumes but elated to be at large, driven to the nearest town, jumping a goods train bound for the capital…

One lunchtime, about three weeks into the term, Molly was sitting in a corner of the canteen buried in one of her film books while hordes of kids lined up with trays to collect bread rolls and smelly fish. She was contemplating a hunger strike which given the food on offer would be no hardship!

Suddenly Vanessa, in showstopping tennis gear and leather jacket, appeared at the door. She looked about her, spied Molly alone and made a beeline for her. "Hey, Molly, time to get your head out of your dusty ol' books! Ange, Nat and I are skipping classes this afternoon and hitting the village. It'll be neat. You ought to come."

Without waiting for a response she breezed off to the front of the lunch queue and, ignoring all complaints, leaned over the counter, helped herself to a low-fat yoghurt and strode purposefully towards "her" table.

Daniela, who had been approaching and had overheard Vanessa's invitation, hurried towards Molly. "Don't go with them," she cautioned. "Vanessa doesn't care what happens. She's so rich. Her mother's had three husbands. You could be expelled."

Expulsion!! That was the solution. Why in heaven's name hadn't Molly thought of it herself? Without a second's delay she got up, crossed to Vanessa and accepted the invite while Daniela, puzzled, withdrew.

Outside the village café, which reeked of Gauloises, Molly was introduced to two local boys, Jean and Michel, both of whom were around seventeen.

Jean, the dishier of the pair, looked Molly over and smiled. "Is she invited to the Hotel California?" he enquired.

"Uh-huh! Not yet. We don't know whose side she's on yet, do we, Molly?" replied Vanessa. Mystery laid on with a trowel!

They all grinned in response except Molly. Shrugging her shoulders, she wandered away across the cobbled square, which reeked of garlic and gasoline, towards the *bureau de poste*. Her pockets were bulging with letters to her parents.

Mr Darly was the name of the postmaster. He was as mottled and red as a strawberry. "You're new, aren't you?" he asked.

Molly nodded.

"Has nobody warned you that the village is out of bounds to students during the week," he plonked Molly's requested stamps on to the counter as he spoke, "and that those young chaps your pals are always flirting with are out of work?"

Molly peered out at the café, where a group of old men sat drinking pastis and the boys were lounging against bikes. So what if they were unemployed? Her dad was as well. The boys seemed OK. "Out of work" wasn't necessarily something to be ashamed of.

"Where's the cinema?" She had decided to ignore the other topic. In any case, access to the pictures was her most pressing question.

"Nearest one is forty-five minutes by bus."

"Forty —!" But before Molly could complete the

expression of her dismay the door burst open and her three room-mates dived screaming into the shop.

When Molly returned to her dormitory from Madame Savère's office she had received a "very serious warning", but had not managed to get herself expelled. Watched by Daniela she threw herself miserably on to her bed and buried her head under her pillows.

"I warned you," chided Daniela as she crossed the dorm to Molly.

"You don't understand! I *want* to be kicked out."

"Why?"

But Molly was unwilling to discuss her parents' separation, or to mention the stream of letters she'd written to her dad, not one of which he'd answered.

At that moment Vanessa swanned in, announcing loudly, "*Molly Greenfield was buying stamps*! How about it, guys? She didn't even have the guts to stand up for where she'd been."

"I *was* buying stamps!"

"Well, *we* got two weeks' detention, so it's up to you to deliver our messages to the café."

"I don't want to get involved."

"You have no choice."

Molly delivered the notes. It seemed simpler. And so what if she got caught? She'd be sent home.

Winter drew on. Molly's relationship with her room-mates grew morose. Even well-meaning Daniela Lubicz kept her distance. She wanted no part in Molly's self-destructive ambition.

Molly began skipping classes. She passed the hours meandering through the forest where the earth was mushy with fallen leaves or holed up in the dormitory, scribbling furiously in notebooks. Words and stories became her companions.

One morning, passing through a gate, she found herself in a walled garden. There were flowerpots on the ground, forks and rakes leaning against a greenhouse. Everywhere was still. Frosted foliage crunched under her boots. The glasshouse glinted in the milky sunlight. She went inside, perched against a copper heating pipe and began a letter to her dad.

"No classes?" a deep, dark voice enquired, breaking into the world of her written thoughts. Molly looked up and saw a tall, aging figure in muddied clothes and wellington boots.

She hadn't heard the old gardener's footfall. Quick as a flash she stuffed the stationery into her anorak. "I've got 'flu," she lied.

"Is that so?" The old man peered in disbelief, but smiled with watery eyes. "Too sick to lend a hand?"

She shook her head.

"Heave ho, then! I'm Mr Beauchamps, by the way." He passed her a trowel.

Outside she hacked at the hard earth and hesitantly, in response to his questions, began to talk. She was taking a risk by confiding in him, a stranger, as though they were old friends.

A few days later she was summoned to Madame Savère's office. This time she was offered tea and *madeleines* and directed to an armchair.

"I was thinking of signing you up for our Action Service Programme, Molly. Visits to the elderly in the village at weekends."

Molly eyed the headmistress with suspicion.

"It'll give you an opportunity to mix with a wider circle, forget your own problems for a while." Madame Savère waited for a response. None came. "You are your own worst enemy, Molly."

"No, I'm not!"

"Then get involved in one of our group activities. Take an interest in others. Skipping classes will get you nowhere, nor will indulging in self-pity."

Molly felt her skin begin to go pink.

"Self-pity is negative and tedious. Is that how you wish to be regarded?"

Tears stung Molly's eyes. She bowed her head.

"What news of your father?"

The question caught her by surprise.

"Has he replied to any of your letters?"

"He's busy…" It was a curt and feeble response but she was unable to admit the truth.

"Would you like to talk about it?"

"There's nothing to say."

Madame Savère sighed, rolling a biro between her fingers. "I shan't expel you; you are wasting your time. I want you to participate, find companions, Molly. Contribute. There lies your mainstay. No one else can do it for you."

Alone in the loos, Molly splashed her face with cold water and inspected the blotched image staring out at her from the mirror. If they wouldn't expel her then she'd bloody well run away! Self-pitying! It wasn't her fault that her dad hadn't answered her letters! She was missing him and she didn't want to talk about it, except maybe to Mr Beauchamps. Was that so terrible?

One of the lavatories alongside her flushed and to her horror Daniela Lubicz appeared from behind the closed door. Molly fiddled with the soap.

"I hope she told you what a pain you're being." Honest and to the point, that was Dan! She spoke with a clipped accent which made her sound like a Russian spy, but she was good-natured. "Why don't you want to make friends?"

Suddenly Molly remembered Jenny and all the confidences they used to share. She felt miserable remembering England and the good times she'd enjoyed. She felt a million light years away from home. "Where are you from?" she asked Daniela.

"Butrymowicze."

"Wherever is that?"

"A remote part of Poland. I live on a farm with my brother and granddad."

"Where are your folks?"

"They're dead."

Molly stared incredulously at Daniela. "Shoot!" Was all she managed to say.

Daniela began to run water into the basin. "They died when I was small."

Molly considered the enormity of such information for a moment. "My dad's left," she confided. "It's a bit like he's died."

"Is that why you are trying to get sent home?"

"Mum and me moved to be near him. Now he's gone. We don't know where."

Dan, watching Molly intently, approached and hugged her.

After her talk with Dan, Molly stopped skipping classes. She couldn't have explained why, exactly. Somehow she felt less isolated. When she recounted her meeting with Madame Savère to Mr Beauchamps he said, "If you don't fancy the Action Service p'raps we could think up something else. She's right about having a project. Keeps your mind off your worries."

It was a Saturday and Vanessa's mum and second

stepdad came to take her out. She invited the others along, including Molly, who considered the gesture pretty generous – but said no thanks anyway. Ange and Nathalie leapt at the opportunity – anything to be liberated from Trouvai for the day. Dan had booked to go horseriding, so she also refused. Molly was left alone at the college, which was fine by her.

She set out on one of her long rambles, choosing a track which skirted a mountain stream, and crossed it by a wooden bridge. Once on the far bank she found that the path led her through a tangle of brambles to a clearing where she came upon an amazing old building.

Originally it must have been a hotel – remote, but Molly couldn't imagine what other purpose it might have served. It didn't take Philip Marlowe to see that the place had been empty for aeons; there were ferns sprouting like shrubs from the gaps in between the stones of the walls and a vine, leafless but not dead, climbing alongside the wooden door.

Molly decided to take a look inside. She pulled and pushed at the door, which was bolted from inside. She rammed her shoulder hard against it, which really hurt, but, worm-rotten though it was, it wouldn't budge. The windows, curtained with grimy muslin, were also locked.

Around the back she spotted a broken pane at first-floor level and scouted about in search of something to stand on. There were several discarded cider barrels brimful with rain water, too heavy to move, and a bench lying on its side. The legs of the bench were decomposing and even if they hadn't been it wasn't high enough.

Eventually she gave up and hurried back in search of the one person who might know the building and who might even have a key.

Mr Beauchamps was planting onions in the plot beyond his cottage. "You look pleased with yourself," he said.

"I've discovered somewhere brilliant!"

Four

"The Hotel California."

Molly recognized the name at once. It was a song recorded by The Eagles. Yes, she knew that, but she'd heard it used somewhere else recently. Then it dawned on her! It was the place Jean, Vanessa's unemployed friend from the café, had mentioned. Where she, Molly, hadn't been invited. Well, here she was, tracing its maze of rooms, attempting to read its scrawled graffiti. She made out the words "Welcome to the Hotel California."

Must be their hideout! A dangerous sanctuary with zonking great holes in the floorboards!

So, after all the hassle of breaking in, this apparently abandoned building wasn't her own discovery. Molly didn't feel deflated – on the contrary, ideas were careering through her brain like cars on a race track.

"Years since anyone's been near this place!" Mr Beauchamps' voice rang through the dusty corridors. He was humming to himself in the room beneath her, picking his way through the rubble. She heard the scraping of furniture. He was tidying up!

When she'd returned here with him earlier his behaviour had been curious. He had obviously recognized the place and had struggled hard to conceal a quiver in his voice, but Molly had detected his emotion. It was as though he were rediscovering a cherished possession.

"Must be twenty years since anyone's set foot in here!" he called from below.

Molly glanced about, considering the evidence which proved him wrong: a cracked compact disc, candle grease on the floorboards, stacks of beer bottles, cigarette stubs, semi-burnt logs in the grate, cushions, chewing gum... She crossed to a moth-eaten blanket and lifted it to reveal a portable stereo system. Bound to be Vanessa's. Not as sophisticated as the one she kept in the dorm, but sufficient for "sounds" on a temporary basis.

Hotel California. Cool name – she liked it.

Was there any electricity? Didn't appear to be. They'd have to rig something up, if she could persuade them to—

"Molly!" Mr Beauchamps was approaching the stairs.

For the time being it would be wiser if he continued to believe the building was unoccupied. Not that she wished to trick him... Only until she had persuaded him to... She scooted to the top of the stairs to head him off.

"On my way!" she called.

Dusk was falling as they left the place. The evening air had a chill in it. Molly wrapped her windcheater firmly about her. She gazed back at the building and then turned to look at the old man at her side, wondering what memories the place held for him.

And then, as though in answer to her unspoken question, he said softly, "When I was a lad, living in the village, the college used this place for dances. I first caught sight of my wife in there, God rest her soul! She was on a stage, singing – a pupil about your age. Later, she became the college music teacher. The stage has gone now, of course." He fell silent.

Molly made no response, preferring not to intrude

upon his memories. But his words gave form to the idea hatching within her. There had been a stage. The building had been used for dances. Why not again?

It was the perfect location, sufficiently remote from the college to remain a secret (until the time for disclosure was ripe), yet close enough to be accessible.

She glanced upwards. Her breath rose like smoke in the cold air. The first star of the evening glimmered brightly. They stepped away from the building and the ground felt crisp and hard under her feet.

"We could rebuild the stage…"

"Rebuild what stage?" His thoughts had drifted elsewhere.

"Create our own cinema. Our own dance hall."

"Good Lord!"

"Good to have an interest, you told me."

"I hadn't envisaged something quite so ambitious. You mean people singing and dancing?"

"A club. Live music, films. My dad could run it—"

"Whoa! Slow down, Molly!"

"No, listen. It'd give Dad a regular job. He could live in the village."

"Sounds grand, but…"

They were emerging from the brambles, towards the bridge. The moon shone brightly in front of them now. Mr Beauchamps paused to catch his breath.

"We'll start with a benefit concert," Molly continued. "All proceeds would go to running it as an arts centre."

Without Mr Beauchamps' encouragement Molly knew she might never get the project moving. And suddenly it meant everything in the world to her. It was as though her family's future lay there too.

"Dad'll do it – I know he will. It'll make him feel wanted again."

"We'd have to clean it up…"

That wasn't an objection. *He was actually considering it!*

They were wending their way alongside the stream. The water burbled softly at their side.

"And what will the staff think?"

"We'll run it. Us and—"

"I'd have to clear it with Madame Savère. Don't want to lose my job."

"No! Please, Mr Beauchamps, not yet. Let's surprise her."

They walked in silence for a while. He was mulling it over.

"Nothing I'd like more, Molly, than to see the place in use again, but we'd have to inform Madame Savère."

"Let's sell tickets to all the parents and *then* tell her. It'll be a brilliant surprise!"

"We'd need help for the renovations…"

"I know exactly who to ask."

He was amused by her secrecy and impressed by the strength of her enthusiasm. Her suggestion of bringing the old building back to life pleased him more than he cared to admit.

That evening Molly wrote to her dad, begging him to visit. She needed his feedback. She'd heard nothing from him since he'd kissed her goodbye all those weeks ago.

She decided against confiding in her mum. That could wait until Christmas. Christmas! She couldn't bear to contemplate it.

On the following Saturday evening Molly paid the Hotel California a second visit. It was, as she had anticipated, alive and buzzing. Gathered together in the upstairs room were Vanessa, Angela, Nathalie, Jean and Michel.

"Who the hell invited *you* here?" exclaimed Vanessa when Molly appeared at the door.

The others, startled by her intrusion, remained silent.

"I've had a brilliant idea!" And right away, almost without pausing for breath, Molly outlined her plans for the club and its opening benefit concert.

Their faces were a study.

"You gotta be kidding!" said Vanessa, always the voice of the gang. "This is our pad, not yours!"

"I'm not trying to take it over, honest! There's real potential here. We – we could create something amazing. There'd be no more "out of work" stuff. Plenty for everyone."

They were staring at her incredulously.

"A benefit concert!" Jean alone was rolling the idea around as though testing it.

"Is this the kinda junk you scrawl in your notebooks!" Vanessa's words were derisory but secretly she fancied the subversive nature of the scheme. The trouble was, she couldn't admit it because it hadn't been her suggestion.

Molly waited, confident they'd succumb. Well, fairly confident.

The room looked inviting. The fire was crackling, a Guns 'n' Roses tape was playing on the deck, sausages were sizzling on the open fire. Suddenly her certainty diminished. Why should they want to change? And no one was shouting. "Hey, Molly, let's do it!" She hadn't reckoned on this sort of reaction.

"My dad's a brilliant musician. He'll put it together for us." She'd counted on them *jumping* at it. After all, it would break every rule in the college book. That in itself should be sufficient to excite Vanessa. The others – the girls at least – would follow automatically.

If they refused to come aboard, that was it. Vanessa had said it. The Hotel California was their place, not hers. She couldn't hijack it. She needed them.

"He could bring musicians…"

"Your old man's got his own group then, has he?" Jean, at least, was impressed.

"No, but he gigs with heaps of guys—"

"I play the guitar."

"Hardly!" mocked Vanessa.

"Yeah, I do! Sure, better, if I could afford one." Jean again. Molly beamed at him encouragingly. "Maybe Dad could teach you." If she could persuade Jean, then Vanessa might agree. After all, in Vanessa's perverse, arrogant way, she was nuts about Jean.

"Dad could show us how to run things, and then when the place starts making money, you guys could take over. It'd give you jobs. The benefit's for the unemployed."

"The unemployed!" This *definitely* wasn't a subject that interested Vanessa.

"Cool it, Van. I think it sounds neat."

"I don't see why anyone should do anything for the unemployed."

Jean, at Vanessa's side, coughed and lit a cigarette.

"If we're going to organize a benefit concert you've got to have a reason for the benefit," explained Molly patiently.

"An arts centre, you told us. Screen all the latest movies…"

"I was thinking we might kill two birds with one stone. Jean and Michel need work, my dad's unemployed—"

"You said he was a musician." Angela was growing impatient. And the sausages were turning black. She crawled across the floor and began poking at them with a fork. "I thought you were watching these," she said to Michel.

"He is," said Molly.

"Yes, he is," confirmed Nathalie.

"No, I mean he *is* a musician. My dad. I'm talking about my dad."

"Well, he can't be all that great if he's unemployed!" Nathalie rejoined.

"He's brilliant! Loads of good creative people suffer lean times. Listen, let's just forget the whole thing. No big deal." Molly turned, and then stopped. Her temper was about to lose her the one thing that had been keeping her going.

"Molly!" She turned at the sound of Jean's voice. "It's a real cool idea. I love it!"

He wasn't sending her up. She could see that. Her face broke into a grin.

"So do I," hastened Vanessa.

"And the old place definitely needs a coat of paint," put in Michel. It was the first time Molly had ever heard his voice. It was gentle and, judging by the way he was smiling, so was he.

Molly, standing in the middle of the seated bunch, looked from one to the other. "So, we're on then, are we?"

"You bet!" shrieked Vanessa, leaping to her feet. Within seconds they were all hugging and dancing.

Work began the following week. Jean borrowed ladders and masonry equipment from his dad, who was a plasterer. He suggested asking "the old man" to lend a hand but that met with no support.

"We've got to keep this between ourselves," counselled Vanessa, making the decisions once more.

"Top secret. If Madame Savère finds out she'll stop us," seconded Molly. It was sound reasoning and dangerous fun, which appealed to Vanessa.

While the others slept, Molly, aided by torchlight, jotted down ideas and scribbled page after page to her dad, in the hope that one letter would grab him.

Dad, if you can't visit, please be there for Christmas.

One night, she was so engrossed that she didn't hear Daniela creeping across the slumbering dorm. It was the rush of cold air against her warm flesh that broke her concentration. "Oh, hi, Dan!" she said weakly. "Did I disturb you?"

Daniela stared sullenly.

"Could I have the duvet back, please, Dan? It's freezing."

Daniela released the cover and Molly tucked it swiftly around her. "What are you staring at?"

"I think you're mean!"

"For Heaven's sake, why?"

To Molly's amazement, Dan climbed into the bed. "You're all up to something," she whispered, "and I want to know what it is."

"We are, but we need you too."

"Then why haven't you said anything?"

"I didn't want you to turn us down. It's a bit risky."

"How, risky?"

"We're organizing a benefit concert and we want you to be social secretary."

In the torch-lit darkness Daniela's eyes widened with interest.

"It's a huge and amazing secret. You mustn't breathe a word. Promise?"

"Promise. Now, *tell me*!"

And so whispering into the wee small hours, buried beneath a cave of bedding, Molly outlined a million dreams. By the time she rolled over to invite Dan's opinion, Daniela was sound asleep.

Five

Daniela flicked through the pages of her diary. "Open Day is held in the spring. If your event —"

"Ours —"

"— is to succeed, the California needs to be renovated by then."

Molly frowned.

"Molly, Open Day is the only day in the year when all the parents descend upon this forgotten mountainside. They fly in from everywhere. They won't do that twice, not even to hear your dad play the best jazz in Europe."

Now she was catching Dan's drift. "You mean, hold our benefit on the same evening?"

"Gosh, Molly, sometimes you're dreadfully slow!"

"We'll work evenings."

Before Daniela could list the impracticalities of working evenings in the middle of winter in a barn of a building without electricity or running water, Molly had scooted off in search of Jean and Michel.

They kitted out the California with metres of piping rigged to a pump, which delivered fresh water from the stream. Storm lamps and a camping stove provided light and heat; working evenings became feasible.

With Molly as Girl Friday, the boys bashed holes, filled plastic bags with debris, swept and scrubbed. Each evening, when they were too bushed to lift another nail, they escorted her back through the bitter winter to her dorm.

She knew the risks and covered her tracks proficiently. If she were caught, she would be expelled, the very thing she'd been angling for all term! But as each day passed Molly's yearning to be kicked out grew fainter. If she were expelled her dad's jazz would never reach the California, and there would be no cinema for Trouvai.

There were some days when the bursts of enthusiastic labour ground to a halt.

"Hey guys, we're broke again!" Money, or the lack of it, was their toughest hurdle.

Jean's dad contributed and Jean, who had been having a rotten time at home, was forced to admit that his old man was magnanimous. Mr Beauchamps also dug into his savings regularly, against Molly's wishes, but the main source of revenue was Vanessa, whose coffers proved bottomless and whose generosity was an equal match.

However, crazy as Vanessa was about the scheme, when it came to the nitty-gritty grind, her interest was zero!

On the afternoon Molly handed her a scrubbing brush, Vanessa gave her a withering look and declared, "I never lift anything heavier than a mascara brush! Well, maybe I could handle a toothbrush!"

This caused gales of laughter from the gang and Molly began to realize that something more glamorous than toil was required to maintain Vanessa's enthusiasm.

As well as financial assistance, Mr Beauchamps donated all his spare time. He never discussed it, but Molly had a hunch that the project meant a great deal to him.

On the last morning of term she discovered him at the California. He was wandering to and fro, admiring the freshly painted surfaces.

"You're making a fair old job of it," he said.

"Jean and Michel did the bulk. If Dad comes at Christmas —"

"*When* he comes, Molly."

"— I'm going to chat to him about the music. Ask him to find us some old songs, create a theme for the benefit."

"I'll give it some thought myself, shall I?"

"That'd be swell. Merry Christmas, Mr Beauchamps!"

She handed him a scruffy parcel containing woollen gloves purchased in the village and retreated discreetly. A lump came into her throat when she glanced back and caught sight of him standing there alone in the centre of the hall with his memories. She promised herself that she would come up with something wonderful for him to do at the benefit. That would be the neatest thank-you she could offer him.

Christmas, for Molly, was about being with her folks. It had always been like that. But now everything had changed.

She received a card from Jenny (one of those loony stand-up ones), telling her all the news from England and finishing with the line "Roger Tanret still loves you!" Instead of cheering Molly up and making her laugh, it made her feel bluer.

She kicked herself for having expected her dad. He hadn't written, hadn't answered her letters, hadn't given her any reason to count on him, yet she had kept faith and always believed he'd turn up, even when her mum had said, "Don't bank on it, Moll; don't expect him."

Christmas day dragged by. They stayed at home and

ate turkey. There was plenty for seconds but Molly had no appetite. She mooched about, browsed through the books Alice had hidden in her stocking and stared out of the window, all the while glancing at the unclaimed present beneath the tree: the Nina Simone compilation she'd bought for her dad at the Virgin megastore.

"Cheer up, sweetheart! You've walked about with that long face ever since you got out of bed this morning."

"Don't nag, Mum."

"I won't nag if you don't behave like such a party pooper."

Molly gathered up the book in her lap and disappeared to her room.

Always, when they had a disagreement, Alice appeared at Molly's door, but this time she didn't knock. She marched in and plumped herself at the foot of Molly's bed. She didn't speak, she stared.

Molly tugged at her hair, trying to ignore her mum.

"Have you stopped to consider?"

"What?"

"That I might be… as well…"

"Might be what?"

"Wishing your father was here with us, sad that we're not a family, the way we used to be."

Molly said nothing.

Alice waited and then added softly, "Didn't you ever think that I might be missing him? That I may have been hoping he would spend Christmas with us?"

Still Molly made no response, but she began to feel uneasy.

"What I'm saying, Molly, is that it's high time you thought about those around you. Your self-pity is tedious."

Alice rose and departed, leaving Molly alone, dumbfounded.

Self-pity! Those words again!

Molly lay awake for ages, tossing and turning, ruminating on her mum's words. They were true. She hadn't been thinking about her mum at all.

The good news was that her mother obviously still loved her dad, so her dream of bringing her parents back together wasn't an unrealistic fantasy. Once her dad found a job, he'd come back to them. Alice's words, right? *If she could succeed with the benefit, get the club going* … Somehow she had to find a way of talking to him face to face. But how?

It was about then, lying in silence, that she heard a key in the lock. She sat up, perfectly still, needing to reassure herself that she wasn't dreaming. There were footsteps in the hall.

Molly sprang out of bed. As he opened her door she was upon him, hugging him with all the strength she possessed.

"I knew you'd come," she whispered. "I knew you wouldn't let me down."

In the kitchen the following morning Molly couldn't stop yakking. Laying the knives and forks on the table, she was jabbering fifteen to the dozen. Her parents weren't saying a word. Her dad sat listening while her mum rustled up a Boxing Day special: scrambled eggs, bacon, tomato, fresh parsley from the market and warm *croissants* from the *boulangerie*.

Her dad looked whacked. He'd barely opened his mouth, but then she was so busy rabbiting on about the benefit that he'd hardly been given a chance.

As she spoke, outlining the achievements and the California schedule for the coming months, it crossed her mind that keeping secret a scheme which meant so much to her might have hurt her mum. Alice was disconcertingly quiet, chopping and rinsing things, moving between the stove and the sink, hardly showing her face to either Molly or Molly's dad.

Molly didn't stop to think about it; she was too intent on engaging her dad's interest.

She had to persuade him to take part. That, above all, before he left again. There was no knowing when they might see one another again. If she didn't extract a promise from him this morning all her plans might be in vain.

She blathered on, watching his face, searching for signs, gauging his interest, dreading that he'd dismiss the whole thing.

"My first idea was to turn it into a cinema. Then Mr Beauchamps mentioned how it'd been used for dances, so I thought, let's do that again. Let's have an opening benefit with dancing."

Peter laughed. Alice drew close to the table and handed him his eggs. "Thanks. You've got it all worked out, eh, Moll?"

"I'll need your advice for lots of it. Thanks, Mum." Her breakfast was placed in front of her. It smelt delicious. She began to eat.

"What does the college think about all this?" Alice returned to the stove to fetch a plate for herself.

Molly knew from the tone of her mum's voice that she was upset.

"We'll tell them when it's ready," she replied.

Alice turned back from the draining board and looked at Molly. Her eyes were watery and blazing. Was she crying, angry, or what? Molly was confused. Peter began forking food from his plate. Alice was directly behind him so he couldn't see her face. No doubt, though, he'd detect the edge in her voice.

"What if they say no?"

"They can't, Mum. Not once the tickets are sold. It's for a good cause. The main thing is..." Molly took a deep breath, "we need someone for the music." Her eyes rested on her dad. He was forking up tomato. He said nothing. There was silence for a heartstopping moment. It seemed like forever. She wondered if he'd been listening to anything she'd said.

"One of the guys is learning the guitar..." she continued.

"There are plenty of good musicians about, Molly. Putting them together, knowing how to run things, that's another skill. How about letting me have a go?"

He'd said it! Taken her seriously! Offered to run the show! She could hardly believe it. She was on her feet, scooting from the room. "I'll get my notes!"

"Don't make her promises you can't keep," said Alice, crossing to the table.

Peter made no response.

"She's serious. She'll build her hopes. The staff are already disappointed. Read her report. She's not participating."

Peter put his knife and fork down on his plate. "Maybe they don't see what they should be encouraging."

"Have a word with her, but please don't be thoughtless. She'll bank on you, Peter."

Molly, unseen by both, had appeared in the doorway clutching her precious notes.

"Give me a break, Alice!" Her father's words. The anger and resentment which lay behind them reached right inside Molly's heart. So, too, did the bleakness in her mother's face. Unwilling to watch any more, she retreated to her room.

It was there her father found her.

He was wearing his overcoat and a pale blue scarf hung from between his fingers.

"I'll be on my way, Moll," he said.

She stared hopelessly at her papers spread out across the bed.

"Your mother doesn't want me making promises I can't—"

"The benefit's months away! You could keep it free. And if that first dance goes well we could make it a regular spot – something we could do together, Dad." She lifted her eyes towards him. She felt sure he wanted to say yes. They understood each other, right? How could it not appeal?

"Let me think about it, eh?"

"It'd give you a chance to have your own band… play the music you like."

"Moll, listen." He tossed the scarf on to the bed and drew close. "It's a terrific idea." He took her gently by the elbows and swung her body to face him.

"But…?"

He led her to the bed, sat her down and seated himself by her, pushing aside papers. The brief clearing of his throat signalled his discomfort. She recognized it instantly.

"Your mother's a bit concerned about your studies. Seems you're not pulling your weight, not putting your mind to the right things."

Molly said nothing, read his words as an elaborate refusal. Her dream began to ebb away.

"Everyone's expecting a lot of you."

"I don't know why." Her voice was low and unresponsive.

"Because you're bright. You don't want to get kicked out, do you?"

"Oh, Dad, please say yes. Even if you only agree to the opening night. Please, let's just give it a go."

He weighed up her words while watching her. "What

if I were to make you a promise?"

She lifted her face, regarding him expectantly.

"Work hard for the rest of the year, make your old man proud of you, and I'll play the opening night."

"You will?"

"If you get permission."

"You don't believe I can do it?"

"I'll bet my last buck you can. You follow your dreams, Moll. That's what counts." He rose, gathering up his scarf, and was on his way.

She had no idea when she would see him again, but she had elicited the cherished promise. "We'll meet again soon, won't we, Dad? To organize things."

"You bet. See ya, sweetheart!" He was by the door, smiling. Laughing. He was on his way.

"I'll make you proud of me, Dad – promise." She smiled too when he winked, then watched him disappear beyond the room.

If only she could have persuaded him to stay.

Six

"You are so late!" cried Daniela as Molly bustled into the dorm and flung her backpack on to her bed.

"Our car was playing up."

"Don't you feel embarrassed driving in that wreck?" Nathalie had been watching Molly's arrival through the window.

" 's only a car." Molly was standing in the middle of the room, glancing about, toying with the idea of going directly to the California. Or should she postpone it until the following day? It was almost evening. "Anyone seen Jean or Michel?"

"I'm keeping Jean waiting."

"Whatever for?"

Her room-mates were lolling together on Vanessa's bed. At the foot of it sat a snazzy portable TV, slender as a playing card – one of Vanessa's numerous Christmas gifts. Vanessa was looking fantastic, posing as though on a tropical island, brown as a berry. "I had to spend New Year's Eve in Bermuda. With my *father*! Can you imagine?" she moaned.

"Weren't you pleased to see him?" Molly was still hovering in the centre of the room.

"Hardly my scene!" She stroked the golden glow of her skin. "I went to the beach and hungered for Jean."

"Then why haven't you called him?"

"It's cooler if he misses me."

"Why?" Molly crossed to her corner and began dragging clothes and books out of her backpack.

"You're so naïve, Molly."

"Maybe."

"How was your Christmas, Molly?" It was Angela asking – Angela, looking uncomfortable in too-tight jeans. She must have spent the holidays stuffing herself with pudding.

Molly, busy with sweatshirts, kept her back to the others. "Er, I was with my dad. We spent *days* going through the plans for the California." Why was she exaggerating about the time she'd spent with her father? Because it hurt to listen to the others. Their home lives seemed so much less fraught than her own jumbled existence.

"What did he reckon?"

"He came up with a terrific idea for you, Vanessa."

"You talked about *me*?"

"Well, you, Nathalie and Ange." Molly plumped herself on her bed. Hands buried, she crossed her fingers. She always crossed her fingers when she was about to tell a lie – although this wasn't exactly a lie. *If* her dad had stayed and *if* she'd talked it through with him, he'd have agreed that it was a smashing way to keep the girls excited about the project. She preferred to see it as *telepathic collusion* between her dad and herself.

"What about me?" Daniela asked.

"What sort of a terrific idea?"

"You're the Social Secretary, Dan, remember? He doesn't need to think up something for you. You've got a rôle."

Daniela smiled and nodded. She was relishing the prospect of being Social Secretary, looking forward to the responsibility.

"So, what's the terrific idea?"

"You three are the back-up."

"*Back-up?*"

Vanessa's tone tickled Molly. She knew Vanessa was going to jump for joy when she heard. "Back-up vocals. Along the lines of Diana Ross and the Supremes."

"Diana Ross!"

Molly pictured the glittery dresses swimming about in her room-mate's imagination.

"Wow! Your dad *is* brilliant!"

"He thought you'd like it." Molly, highly amused, went back to her unpacking.

On the Saturday she set off with Mr Beauchamps. They were carrying tubers for planting.

"I've thought of a theme."

"And what might that be then?" He was huffing and puffing, bending and rising, rubbing at his back after every few dahlias.

"A prohibition club in Chicago. Jean and Michel can be the gangsters, Vanessa, Ange and Nathalie will be their molls. Dad – that's easy, the bandleader; and you, Mr Beauchamps, the star of the show, will be Al Capone!"

He roared with laughter. "You have a wild imagination, Molly."

"No, really; we'll decorate the hall so it becomes an illicit bar in prohibition Chicago. Where we live in Paris, an exterior wall of the building has been painted with palm trees. They look kinda 3D. Instead of living in a street the building looks as though it's in a tropical garden. Really neat."

"We French call it *trompe l'oeil*, Molly."

"Well, over Christmas, I kept looking at it. I thought we could do that at the California – paint the walls with early American skyscrapers. Have you seen the film *The Untouchables*?"

Mr Beauchamps, transfixed by her enthusiasm and her flights of fancy, shook his head. "Never heard of it."

"It's set in Chicago. Al Capone's patch. We'll recreate the windy city. You'll knock 'em dead as Al Capone!"

The gang were thrilled. Molly's idea ignited their imaginations. As the weeks and then months rolled by the California was gutted, renovated and transformed.

Then the invitations were designed, the accompanying letter written and photocopies made. All of these were Dan's department, while Molly volunteered for the unenviable task of slipping each letter into its envelope.

The remaining free time was given over to rehearsing the girls, now christened The Van-tones at Vanessa's suggestion, agreed to by everyone except Angela, who preferred the Angel-tones.

"The name isn't the issue. Let's rehearse!" cajoled Molly.

The boys looked on, cheering as Molly (wearing a Spielberg-styled director's cap) taught the girls a series of routines. Although she was no dancer herself, Molly adored choreographing all the fancy numbers. "The secret's in the way you move!" she encouraged the girls as they tap-tapped their soft-shoe rhythms.

Under normal circumstances Molly would have been having a ball, but she hadn't heard from her father. Why hadn't he been in touch?

"Nothing wrong with the way those chicks move!" yelled Jean, who was balanced on a stepladder. Sketched on the wall behind him was his Chicago-version of the Empire State Building. Gangsters, drawn like cartoon figures peeping through windows, were the giveaway. "Dat's how you know it's Chicago and not Noo Yawk!"

Molly was about to pull a face at Jean when she caught sight of the wall. "Hey, that's wild!" she cried.

Michel, buried beneath pyramids of polystyrene, was building props: prohibition-style polystyrene machine guns, outsized dollar bills, hat-check girls and an almost life-sized vintage car, all sticky with fresh paint.

"Some of those windows need to be lit," he called to Jean, referring to the Empire State creation.

"With electrics? But it's not 3D!"

"No! Paint it so it's night and the lights are on!" Michel had been dead keen on the idea of decorating one entire wall with an authentic copy of the Empire State Building, but because "That's New York, not Chicago" his suggestion was shouted down. This was their compromise.

"Gotcha!" Jean went back to his artwork.

Molly turned to the girls. "That's coming on great, Nathalie."

"What we need now is to meet your dad. Talk to him about what songs he'll want."

Molly's heart sank.

"It's crazy rehearsing numbers when we don't know if he'll fancy them." Vanessa's frequent references to Molly's dad weren't complaints – she was really enjoying herself. Even so they unsettled Molly.

"When's he likely to be here, Molly?" It was the third time Nathalie had enquired in as many days.

Molly managed a reassuring grin, then stared at the compact discs spread about the floor. "Real soon, when he's back from his tour."

How much longer could she keep up the bluff?

Later in the day, when everyone had eaten lunch and tidied away the dishes (snappy organization these days at the California!), Molly disappeared into an adjoining room. She could hear the gang through the wall. They were larking about together, rehearsing, singing, playing music. No one had picked up on her insecurity. In less than eight weeks it would be the benefit night. If the replies to all the invitations were positive, the California would be humming with people dancing, enjoying themselves, sharing in the illusion of Prohibition Chicago.

Oh Dad, please make contact!

"You want to tell me what's up?" Mr Beauchamps' voice. Molly, kneeling on the floor, caught sight of his shoes and lifted her head.

He was smiling down at her. "I can't crouch down there. It'll do my old back in."

"There's a chair in the corner. I'll get it for you." She dragged the chair towards him. He sat.

"You want help with those envelopes?"

"I'm fine." She tried to smile but knew she didn't fool him.

"I heard you came first in English. Told your dad?"

She froze. He was too old and canny not to see through things. She fidgeted with the piles of invitations spread out on the floor in front of her. She couldn't look him directly in the eyes. He had worked so hard, contributing a lion's share of his savings to this benefit.

She felt a fraud.

"I've been expecting to hear. He must have... gone on the road..."

"He won't let you down, don't you fear." His words were softly spoken, reassuring.

She felt warm and grateful for his tender confidence.

"I haven't heard," she whispered.

"He was there at Christmas, wasn't he?"

"Yeah, but silence since."

"Too soon to fret, my girl. Now let's get these blasted envelopes out of our hair or we'll have no guests!"

It was Molly who carted the invitations down the hill to the *bureau de poste*, setting off during breakfast when few staff were milling about. She couldn't afford to be spotted – the loaded bag would draw attention. She had even taken the precaution of writing a note: "Due to a swollen ankle, Molly Greenfield will be absent from the first of the morning's sessions." It would be foolish to get caught for such a trifle when so much was at stake. Anyhow, it was only netball, which she detested.

Mr Darly fell about laughing when she heaved the holdall on to his counter. "Running away?" he teased.

"Chance'd be a fine thing!"

"All for your dad, are they?"

Molly might have laughed if the remark hadn't cut so close to the bone. "How much for this lot?"

Mr Darly noted her mood and tempered his accordingly. "Oh, I think we could defer payment for the time being."

Molly stared quizzically.

"You can pay me out of the profits."

"Profits?" she repeated weakly. "How—?"

"Not too many secrets in this village I don't know."

It must have been Jean's dad who had told him. "Promise not to say anything!"

"Mum's the word, Molly."

"Sure you don't want paying now?"

"Anyone who can get those boys working deserves my support. And don't forget to keep me a ticket. Always fancied m'self as a cop from one of those gangster shows on the telly!"

Mr Beauchamps decided to go in search of Molly that

afternoon. Usually it was she who came looking for him, puffing and panting, grinning and yelling, "Mr Beauchamps, I've had a brilliant idea!" But not today. Today it was his turn. He'd seen that troubled look on her face at the California, when he'd mentioned her father and felt she was in need of a friend.

He caught sight of her as she was leaving the library and called to draw her attention. She waved and sauntered across the grass to greet him.

There's the proof, he said to himself. A couple of months ago she would have been charging towards me, blazing with energy.

"Hello, Mr Beauchamps."

"Post that sackful of letters?"

She nodded, shifting gravel with her sneaker.

"Molly, about the costumes…"

"Oh, I… er… haven't sorted anything out yet, Mr Beauchamps."

"I thought we should have a rummage through my spare room. I locked it up after my wife passed away. Hardly opened it since. Lord only knows what's in there. Or have you too much homework?"

"Wouldn't it be better to wait and see if—?"

"I believe we should forge ahead, prepare everything. Then *when* – not if but *when* – your Dad calls you'll be able to reassure him. Everything's ready, you'll tell him. Coming?"

Mr Beauchamps led the way across the soft spring grass. Molly followed. The mountain air blew fresh against her skin.

Once inside his cottage he lit the stove and put the kettle on. "You go and have a browse, if you can get past all those tea chests. I unlocked the room earlier – let the moths out!"

Molly disappeared.

"When did you last speak to your mother?" he shouted, pouring water into the pot.

"Couple of weeks ago."

"Have you written?"

"Of course."

He arranged cups and chocolate biscuits on a tray and carried it through to his sitting room.

"She replies, does she?"

"Mostly."

"Tea's ready when you are."

There was no answer.

He set everything out on the table alongside the phone. Molly's passion for exploring was keeping her occupied. He smiled. She'd be pleased to chat to her mum. And who knew? Mrs Greenfield might have news of Molly's dad. Making contact was the thing. At any rate, it was worth the try.

"I love dressing up!" shrilled Vanessa.

Molly threw open the case and the disintegrating finery tumbled out, reeking of age and mildew. The girls stared in horror.

"Phew! What a pong!" Angela voiced her disappointment.

"Looks like jumble from one of those flea markets!" grumbled Nathalie.

"Never been to one." Vanessa bent to retrieve a fox fur. "Jeez, mothballs!" She crinkled up her nose and averted her face.

Dan, who lived on a farm and had been cured of niceties about odours, said, "It's still got its limbs."

"And head and tail. It's disgusting! How could anyone walk around with a dead animal hanging from their shoulders?"

"Women like Mrs Beauchamps died before Animal

Rights had been invented," explained Molly.

"It's nothing to do with that," continued Nathalie, "I don't care about all that politically correct stuff. It's the mouldy smell I can't stomach. I don't want it near me."

Molly tipped the suitcase on to its side and the clothes spilled across the floor. "Let's leave it to air."

"That fur looks like a dead dog. I'd rather wear boring old grunge than this. Nobody's going to fancy us in this get-up!"

"Molly's just trying to organize things, Ange." Daniela threw Molly a sympathetic glance. "Let's see how we feel about it tomorrow."

"I'm sleeping next door. I don't want to be here when it starts crawling about." Angela peeled her duvet from her bed and disappeared.

"Maybe we can sew new costumes from the good bits or... shoot, I don't know." Molly sighed. Mr Beauchamps was right; she had to keep her spirits lifted. Telephoning her mum had cheered her up.

"What do you think?" she'd asked her, referring to the sample invitation she'd posted several days earlier.

"Peter Greenfield's Sextet... mm... perhaps he can't be there, Molly."

"Have you heard from him?"

"As a matter of fact, we're having a meeting tomorrow with... I'll give him the invitation. I'm sure he'd like to see it. I'll ask him to call you, shall I?"

"That'd be brilliant! Thanks, Mum."

Molly sprawled across her bed now, surveying the ragged array of smelly jumble lying on the floor and wondering what to do with it. What a relief that her dad was finally going to get in touch! With luck and his advice, everything would be settled before the weekend.

A fortnight or so later, when Daniela went to collect her

mail, she was taken aback to find that her pigeonhole was spilling over with letters.

Fearful of being questioned, she stuffed the whole lot into her bag and hurried off in search of Molly.

Molly was equally overwhelmed by the sight. "Please, don't let them all be noes," she cried ripping open the first envelope. When she read the response her face fell like a stone.

"What does it say?"

She handed the letter to Dan, who perused it in silence. "Open the others."

Four refusals, one after the other. *"Thumbs down!"* Each offered a perfectly valid reason why. And then – a flush of luck – six on the trot accepted.

"Whoopee!"

They yowled, they whooped, they all but performed an Indian war dance (they were in the forest a safe distance from prying eyes). Exhausted, they plumped themselves on to the mossy earth and settled back against the trunk of an oak. The early season sun shone in strips through the overhead branches.

"I can hardly believe it."

"Shall we both tell Madame Savère, or would you rather go alone?"

In her excitement Molly had temporarily forgotten her father's silence.

"Molly?"

"You still have to design the poster, Dan, and we need costumes. That's numero uno. No one wants the smelly stuff, so a rethink is called for. Problem is, we haven't a bean. The benefit is currently running on empty. I owe Mr Darly for stamps, Mr Beauchamps has donated a fortune—"

"Molly?"

Silence.

"Madame Savère…?"

"It's far too soon. We've only got six yeses."

During the weeks which followed dozens more positive responses arrived. Life became a delicate juggling act for Molly; calming Dan's anxieties, maintaining a high enthusiasm amongst the gang and studiously avoiding divulging anything to Madame S *until she was sure her dad was coming…*

Why hadn't he made contact?

Mr Beauchamps advised the others to leave her alone. He knew what was troubling her.

April was drawing to a close. On the last Saturday of the month Vanessa announced that she would be out all day. Everyone, particularly Jean, was miffed.

"How can you choose to just go off like that without considering the rest of us? We need you here, Van. These final stages are crucial."

Vanessa refused to argue. She promised to be back for their evening barbecue. When she did return she was laden with costumes. They were so divine she was instantly forgiven.

The mood was one of high elation. Once they were dressed, nobody wanted to take their costume off!

Mr Beauchamps took control. "Better not sit about in them. Too natty to spoil," he said, looking particularly dashing in his Al Capone stripes and spats. It cheered Molly to see him look so good, although she had never doubted that the rôle would suit him – the most benign Al Capone in history!

Angela's dress was too tight and she tugged at it with such desperation that she split the seams. Vanessa shouted at her and Angela ran off and locked herself in the loos.

Molly volunteered to go after her. "Ange, Vanessa

didn't mean anything, honest. Come on, your sausages will get cold," she said to the closed lavatory door.

"They screw up my diet. Go away!"

Not wanting to make matters worse, Molly decided to leave her friend alone. "We're out in the yard waiting for you, whenever you're ready. See you later."

Molly headed back outside. She was in a turmoil. At last she had admitted to herself that Dan was right. She couldn't keep stalling – it wasn't fair on her friends. All the work that had gone into this benefit, all the time and effort they had contributed, the terrific cozzies Vanessa had bought for them… it was time to lay her cards on the table. *Listen, guys, my dad hasn't contacted me. We'll have to go ahead without him.* She would pluck up the courage and say it.

But Life is so weird…

At that crucial moment, as she was making her way through the California's kitchen, she heard a voice enquiring, "Am I at the right place for the benefit?" And Jean's reply, "It's not for another two weeks. Who wants to know?"

She dashed to the door, pausing only to take in the scene: her pals grouped around a fire regarding the handsome stranger, puzzling about who he might be. And then she leapt, kicking over paper plates, spilling ketchup and Coke, in her fervour to reach him. "Where have you been?" she whispered. "I was giving up."

Seven

Her dad ate sausages with them. Angela too. Around the blazing fire he recounted tales of his life on the road. Molly was proud as hell.

Later, while the others tidied away the debris, she grabbed her first moments alone with him. "Ages I've been trying to get hold of you."

"I said I'd be here." He dug into his pocket, pulled out the invitation and studied it.

"Where've you been?"

"Paris."

He must've received her letters then.

"Mum said you've been seeing one another."

"Once or twice. Look at this, Moll: 'Peter Greenfield's Sextet!' You might have made it a trio. I have to pay these guys."

"You will play for us, then?"

"Did you doubt it, my girl!"

"No... no, course not. Dad, any chance that you and Mum —?"

"Come on, Moll; let's sort out the dance routines, then I gotta dash for that train."

Sunday was perfect – a day of musical harmony. It was mindblowing listening to the girls wax lyrical about her dad.

Angela promised that for a man as heavenly as Peter Greenfield she would *definitely* stick to her diet.

Vanessa all but rebuffed Jean, so smitten was she with Peter's charm. "He's *dreamy*! When he put his hands on my ribcage, told me to take a deep breath and hit those high notes, I thought I'd melt. If this becomes a regular date, I'm going to beg him to let me sing with his band."

Molly was nonplussed. She'd never thought of her father in this way. "We're trying to create work for *him*, and for Jean and Michel. Not you, silly!"

Only Dan remained grave. "I am going to Madame Savère and I refuse to be talked out of it."

Molly was slipping sheets of music back into order.

"The benefit is thirteen days away, Molly! Apart from anything else I need to display all my posters around the village."

"She's seeing me tomorrow," replied Molly calmly.

"What? Then our worries are over?"

"They certainly are, Dan."

Madame Savère listened in stony silence as Molly gave her the lowdown. Seated behind her desk, surrounded by neat piles of paperwork and framed photographs, she peered over her tortoiseshell spectacles at the invitation.

Hands tucked into Wranglers, fingers crossed for luck, Molly stood and waited. The silence was growing ominous. Her life, her dreams were hanging in the balance!

"Am I to understand that, without asking anyone's permission, you have sent one of these invitations to every parent?"

Molly nodded.

"Do you have any idea how dangerous that building is?"

"We've renovated it —"

"Who is 'we'?"

"I persuaded the others. They were reluctant —"

"Yes, yes, Molly." Madame Savère flipped the invitation over, glanced at the other side, which was blank, and turned it back. The gesture was impatient. "How many have accepted?"

"Eighty-three. Most are bringing partners, so that's a hundred and sixty-six. Lots still to come."

"Eighty-three…" Madam Savère took a deep breath, attempting to conceal both her sense of admiration and her outrage. "Have any of these parents actually purchased their tickets?"

"Most have."

"And what have you done with the money?"

"Put it in a bank account."

Madame Savère put the invitation firmly on the desk. "You know very well that students are forbidden bank accounts."

"Nothing has been paid to us. We asked specifically. The cheques are made payable to Trouvai Benefit. We know the rules."

"Apparently you do not! Or have you deliberately flaunted them?"

Molly coughed – a short, nervous clearing of her throat, just as her dad always did in a sticky situation.

"I admit that your effort is… commendable, but —"

"It's for a good cause, Madame! A project to help people find work and be useful. It was *you* who told me to get involved and stop feeling sorry for myself. It was great advice!"

"True, but I did not suggest that you ignore our rules."

"What are we going to tell the parents if you cancel? How's it going to look for you and the college?"

"And that, my dear girl, is exactly what you have been banking on, choosing to inform me when you thought it would be too late for me to put a stop to it, is that not so?"

Molly didn't answer. How could she? The old bat had guessed her wheeze exactly.

"And you were right. A cancellation would be unthinkable. You will have your benefit concert —"

Moll flung her arms into the air and spun round. "Whoahey! Thanks, Madame Savère! You're a real sport!" Her sense of joy and relief was so great that she did not notice the headmistress's stony glare.

"— but I will not tolerate you forcing my hand. You are expelled as of the end of this term. I shall inform your mother by mail. Good morning, Molly."

Expelled!

Expelled!

Molly recounted the bones of the interview to her pals. They were horrified.

"What are you going to do?" asked Dan.

"Nothing. I don't want to think about it till after the benefit. If it's a rip-roaring success, maybe she'll change her mind."

"I wouldn't count on it," Angela remarked.

"You want to come to the cottage and call your mum?" offered Mr Beauchamps.

Molly shook her head. "I'll see her at the benefit. Don't let's talk about it any more. I'd rather not."

"We should *all* quit college," suggested Vanessa.

Molly was unable to answer. They were so supportive it made her want to cry. "Let's just make it the best evening ever."

During the days which followed the gang moved into

top gear. They begged the loan of a piano from Madame Garcin, the music teacher, Jean and Michel flyposted Dan's posters in the surrounding villages, Dan persuaded the local paper to contribute a full-page advertisement free of charge, and Angela took up jogging, ate sensibly and lost half a stone.

Molly heard nothing from her mother. Every day she expected to find her in the admin office, ranting and raving, or at the end of a phone bawling her out. Nothing. Molly found it curious, but prayed her luck would hold.

She had to concentrate on the benefit. More than ever the evening needed to be a success – for her dad, for the others and for her own future. She closed her mind to everything else. Not even with Mr Beauchamps would she discuss her feelings about what had occurred.

The truth was, expulsion hurt. Three terms ago it was what she'd been gunning for. But now she had friends, she had created something she believed in, had taken life by the horns, devised a project which excited and inspired people. Her pals, their families, the locals from the village – everyone would enjoy some aspect of it.

And what was the college's response? *Expulsion*!

Her sole consolation was that, if everything went to plan, Jean and Michel and Mr Beauchamps would run the California. They would keep the place open and build the arts centre she dreamed of.

May the fifteenth was a warm, bright Saturday. The views across the mountains were crystal-clear. Parents, families, friends, dogs and nannies arrived by the carload. Some even flew in by helicopter. (Not even Van's folks were that grand!) The open day buzzed with laughter and activity.

The girls saw little of it. They were at the California

hanging balloons, mixing fruit punch Prohibition-style, fixing the final touches for the big evening. Each in turn zoomed back to spend half an hour with her parents, except Dan, whose grandfather had written to say that he would not be coming, and Molly, who had still heard nothing from her mum.

Alice's silence was peculiar. Was she so mad at Molly that she couldn't bring herself to write or phone? Molly couldn't tell, but decided that if she was in for a dressing-down, it was best to leave well alone and hope that her mum's anger would subside. As for her dad: no sweat. *He would be there*.

The most wonderful thing would be if her dad and mum arrived together.

The California was deserted. The gang had disappeared to change into their costumes. Molly picked her way through a maze of microphone wires and climbed up on to the stage. From there she surveyed the hall. Jean and Michel, the paintbrush wizards, had created an ambience which was nothing short of brilliant. Their Chicago-version of the Empire State Building actually *did* light up! In front of it, beyond the sanded dance floor, stood a pair of round tables where life-sized, painted polystyrene gangsters sat – small fat guys in striped suits glued to chairs, smoking polystyrene cigars and looking *real mean*. This was how Molly imagined a film set in Hollywood might look.

What was it her dad had replied when she'd asked him: "You don't believe I can do it?"

I'll bet my last buck you can. You follow your dreams, Moll. That's what counts.

She scanned the cavernous space before her and felt the rising swell of a lump in her throat. And then, to the echoing emptiness and the polystyrene cast of players she rehearsed her speech. "Ladies and gentlemen... thanks for showing – turning up here, that is. I'd like to introduce my dad... Shoot!" She took a deep breath, kicked one dusty sneaker against the other and began again. "Ladies and gentlemen, we are gathered here... Lord! Listen, guys, thanks for turning up. Here's my dad. A great trumpet player. The best. You're going to have a whale of..." The words dried in her mouth. "Oh, hi! I didn't see you there."

Leaning against the door was Jean. He had slicked his hair back and pencilled on a moustache. His suit was striped, baggy and double-breasted. He smiled and approached as far as the dance floor. Here he paused to trip a neat two-step, exposing spats.

Molly, on the stage, burst out laughing. "You look great!"

"You too. Nervous?"

She let out a great sigh. "It's *got* to go well..."

"Yeah."

"Yeah."

"It's shit you got expelled. I mean... What I'm trying to say is, we've had the best time putting all this together, thanks to you, Moll. We might even have paid jobs at the end of it, me and Michel. No longer Those Blokes Without Work. And it's all down to you. You're the one who believed in it. They have no right kicking you out."

Molly was touched by Jean's words, but her emotions were already so charged she could barely bring herself to reply. From outside she heard a peal of laughter. Saved by the bell! "What's that noise?"

Jean hoofed it back to the door and peered out into the failing light. "Our first guests!"

"*Already*!" Molly leapt from the stage. "Music!"

"Hey, Molly, I hope you're going to get out of those sneakers. They look pretty weird with that snazzy frock."

"Where's Dad? Help! We need *music*."

"Don't panic!" And with that Jean began hopping and buzzing like a fly trapped inside a glass, trying to decide what to do first.

"Can't we plug those speakers into something?" Molly asked him.

"Like what?"

"How about Mr Beauchamps' old phonograph? It's over there."

"Don't be dumb, Molly. It's just for show."

Molly ran to and fro, trying to remember where she'd left the shoes that matched her costume while Jean stared out towards the wood. Along the bank came the first couples, sauntering, laughing. "There are about twelve of them."

"Where's Mr Beauchamps?"

"Outside by the trestle tables."

"He'd better start serving the punch. I'll go and grab Vanessa's CD player. Shoot! Where are my *shoes*?"

"Calm down, Molly."

Molly covered her face with her hands, trying to think and, yes, to get a grip on herself. "What time is it? Oh, *where*'s Dad?" Without waiting for a response she was on her way. She caught a glimpse of Mr Beauchamps, looking a million dollars, inviting the arriving guests to "partake of a little refreshment to set the evening off with a bang."

"Molly!" he called. "Any sign of —?"

"All under control, Mr Beauchamps!" And on she ran. Running so fast, she collided with someone approaching from the tree-shaded path.

"Molly!"

It was her mother. Behind her was a small, fat bloke – not anyone Molly knew.

"Can't stop, Mum."

"Molly, you remember Albert?"

Albert? Who was Albert?

"Great to see you, Mum. Gotta go!"

And on she pelted, beating her way through the brambles, snagging her costume, but not seriously and, anyway, it didn't matter. *Where was her dad?* All that mattered was to make music till he got there.

Albert? Albert? And then Molly placed him.

Albert was the owner of the bistro in Paris where her mum was working. *What was he doing here?*

Molly caught a glimpse of her reflection in the glass doors. With her mussed up hair and dishevelled costume, she resembled a scarecrow done up in sequins! At the same moment, and in complete contrast, the Van-tones came slinking down the stairs. Molly felt a wreck but this was not the moment to worry about it.

"Vanessa! Emergency! We need your CD player."

"Where's your dad?"

"Just till he gets here."

They went back to the dorm. Vanessa gathered up an armful of CDs while Angela, looking mindblowingly slender and gorgeous in her restitched, to-die-for dress, picked up the CD player and Molly lurched about under her bed in search of her shoes. She could only find the left one. In the circumstances, because she thought she might be doing a fair amount of running, she was probably better off in her sneakers, even if it looked odd. Once her dad was there and things were rocking she could either hunt for the second shoe or just keep out of sight.

"Why are you taking your new guitar, Vanessa?" asked Nathalie.

"It's a present."

"Who on earth for?"

"Jean…" Vanessa replied shyly.

Molly caught the uncertain pride on her friend's face.

When they arrived at the California there was still no sign of Peter Greenfield or his musicians. There were, though, about two hundred guests milling around the refreshments table. The Van-tones helped Mr Beauchamps serve the punch while Molly and Jean rigged up the sound system.

"It's a bit earlier than we intended, but shall I start selling the raffle tickets?" enquired Dan, head round the door.

"Can't you decide for yourself?" Molly yelled. Dan withdrew tactfully to the droves of expectant guests.

Eventually Jean managed to connect Vanessa's CD to the speakers. They switched the machinery to power and slipped in a Harry Connick Jr disc.

They had music.

At that moment Alice, looking anxious, came to offer help. Without thinking, Molly snapped at her too. "Dad's coming! What's *he* doing here?"

Alice, recognizing Molly's frustration, also returned outside.

"Hey, cool it, Molly," said Jean, wrapping his arm around her shoulder. "He'll be here, your old man. No worries."

But Peter Greenfield and his much-acclaimed, eagerly-awaited sextet never showed up.

The dancing began without him, thanks to Vanessa's endless and varied collection of discs.

People started jiving, rocking to the beat. Jean, with his new guitar, strummed to the recorded music while the Van-tones, *oohing* and *doo-wa-diddying*, swung in their glorious frocks and, much to Molly's amazement, the audience, this motley collection of fashionable parents, began partying. Even her mum was spinning around the floor in the arms of fat Albert.

What had she invited him for?

Molly, still in her grotty sneakers, hid at the back of the stage. Amongst the swirling crowd she picked out the familiar faces. Madame Savère was there with her husband, dancing! Madame Garcin, the music teacher, was circling on her own in a flaming orange flapper costume, waving her arms as though she were sending out Morse code and clearly having a hell of a private party. And, from Lord knew where, Mr Darly had kitted himself out in a US cop's outfit, sergeant status!

More than two hundred people were having a ball, spending money for the centre and the fund for the unemployed. Outside Mr Beauchamps, alias Al Capone, was still loyally flogging his Prohibition punch and Dan, her raffle tickets.

The evening was a rollicking success.

Molly's movie had come to life.

But the one person for whom the whole event had been planned wasn't there to see what she had achieved.

Her job completed, Molly sneaked away.

Outside in the darkness, a clear bright sky above her, she lifted her head to the stars and wept. Hot tears rolled down her cheeks as she ran and ran and ran.

"*Why do you always let me down?*" she cried, alone in the dorm. And without another thought she grabbed the photo of her dad which sat on her bedside table and hurled it with all the fury she could muster against the wall. Tears of glass shattered like her dream across the floor.

She grabbed her backpack from under the bed and threw everything into it. Why wait until the end of term? She had been expelled. Why not split now?

Molly left the building and walked slowly down the winding driveway. A car approached from behind her. Knowing it must've come from the benefit she flagged it down.

"I have to get to Paris," she explained to the couple peering out at her.

"In you get, then."

They asked no questions. It was unexpectedly straightforward.

She slid herself and her backpack on to the shiny leather seat and went to sleep. When she woke up it was early morning and she was in the heart of Paris.

She took a metro to the last address she had for her dad, where she had been sending all the letters, and rang the bell.

He was there. He was wearing his evening suit and looking as though he hadn't slept. But then he often looked like that. Molly stood by the open door and stared up at him.

"I worked hard. I came first in English. I organized the dance. I did what I promised. And you let me down."

"We had a puncture. I've been up all night. I didn't let you down."

"You didn't?"

"I said I'd be there. We tried everything. But there was no spare tyre, no garage, no telephone. I had to leave the guys and van there. I caught the first train back."

Molly smiled gratefully. "I guessed something must've happened."

He crossed from the door into his small room and slung a pullover into a suitcase.

"Where are you going?"

"Poland."

"Poland! What, forever?"

"Two weeks. A jazz festival."

"Take me with you."

"Don't be crazy."

"School's over." (Now wasn't the time to tell him she'd been expelled.) "I won't get in the way, won't cause trouble, honest. I just want to be with you."

Peter continued with his packing. He hated to tell her no. He adored her, but taking her would be foolish, irresponsible. "It's insane, Moll."

She used all the powers of persuasion she could dredge up at this unearthly hour. "I've got my stuff, passport and everything."

"You'd have to ask your mother."

"You can leave her a message." Molly didn't want to speak to her mum. She couldn't deal with the expulsion business now. First she must spend time with her dad, persuade him to come home. Once that had been settled, everything else would fall into place. "Please let me, Dad. I… I need to be with you."

Without looking at her, knowing he was agreeing to something rash, he said, "Come on, then."

Molly rushed at him, a windstorm of relief and gratitude. "Thanks!" she whispered.

Eight

From Warsaw they took a train north to the coastal town of Gdansk. Acres of farmland, punctuated by sprawling industrial zones, flashed past the windows. Their fellow passengers were poorly dressed, in clothes which seemed to come from another era. The expression in their eyes was kindly, but tired and confused. Molly found herself drawn to these strangers.

She was a world away from the comfort of college, her fellow students with their trendy gear, their electronic gadgets and their mountain bikes. These faces were alien to her, pale and drawn. She watched them with uncertainty and curiosity. It seemed odd to consider that this was Daniela's country.

She swiftly put aside all thoughts of Dan and the others; she didn't want to dwell on friends she might never see again. She glanced at her dad. He was sleeping, trumpet at his side, face tilted towards the window. The reflection of the sunlight and shadows from passing trees beyond the window patched his face. She loved him so much. She wondered if he would reject her when she owned up to the fact that she'd been kicked out of college. All for the sake of the benefit – *his* benefit.

If he hadn't left home, none of this mess would have

happened. She had to get her mum and dad back together. Top priority. *Only* priority.

It was late on Sunday afternoon when Molly and her father emerged from the railway station and made their way towards the central square in the heart of the old city of Gdansk.

The sun was shining. It was a warm, bright afternoon. People milled about, walking, sitting, drinking beer. Molly dropped her backpack on to the cobbled stones and surveyed the scene.

"What do you think, my girl?"

Gdansk was like nowhere she'd ever been before – a curious mix of old and new. At one end of the square was the cathedral. Apart from the spire, the entire building was covered in rickety wooden scaffolding. It looked pretty dangerous.

She felt minuscule. Tall, narrow buildings surrounded her, exquisitely decorated with ornate golden sundials, mediaeval figures or clocks. It was a town of giant doll's houses. Molly felt as though she had travelled in a time machine, centuries backwards.

In contrast, hundreds of white plastic tables and chairs spilled from the square's numerous cafés. Fragments of a folk song drifted from across the way and she caught sight of the music-maker, an accordionist. He was dressed in ludicrously short black trousers, which flapped as he drifted between the busy tables, playing tunes and bowing for the coins tossed into his purse. There was something wooden, puppet-like, about his appearance and his movements.

"Well, do you like it here or not?"

"I can't relate it to anything." The place, the atmosphere, the strangeness of it… it was another reality. A Spielberg film set perhaps, or a Hans

Christian Andersen fairy tale.

"Come on, then. Let's get to Pavel's and grab ourselves a bite."

Molly had no objection. She was starving. She hadn't eaten in over twenty-four hours, she'd been so busy with the benefit the day before.

They walked along a narrow lane lined with houses converted into shops. Molly's eye was caught by a jeweller's. In the window was a silver brooch shaped like a butterfly. The wings were crafted from laced silver and the insect body was sculpted out of amber.

"Hey, Dad! Look at that brooch!"

He retraced his steps. "Lovely. Come on, Moll, let's —"

"Mum would love it."

"— be making tracks."

"If it's not too expensive we could buy it for her. Shall I go and ask?" Suddenly it seemed like the neatest idea in the world. A present from them both. Then she wouldn't be angry with Molly for leaving without saying anything and, most importantly, she would know that Peter still loved her.

"Molly…"

"Please, Dad."

"Another time. Pavel will be waiting." The discussion was over. Molly watched her father making his way along the lane. Calling him again would be futile.

Molly's father had been invited to stay with Pavel Kowalski, a saxophonist he had met in the late sixties when they'd both been living in Paris.

Molly's arrival, unexpected as it was, set the household into temporary confusion. Pavel's family was large, his house minute. Never in her life had Molly been in the midst of such a bustling, chaotic family.

There was grandmother Kowalski, Pavel, his large jolly wife Anya, two teenage boys (Radek and Bartosz), a small sister (Agnes) and a tiny baby.

Eventually, it was settled that Molly would share the bedroom belonging to the two boys with her father and Radek and Bartosz would sleep in the living room. She felt awkward about turning them out of their room, but neither boy seemed to care. They accepted it with good humour.

Her dad's enthusiasm in his friend's company was evident. Although it pleased her to see him happy it also unsettled her. Unknown friends made him relax and laugh out loud, whereas at home he had grown morose and short-tempered.

It was as though he were a stranger. Yet he included her. She told herself that her concern was foolish – it came from the strangeness of these new surroundings and her fear of losing him.

Listening to him talking to Pavel, she discovered that his new life in Paris wasn't easy. Work was difficult to come by and she began to realize just how much depended on the jazz festival. This knowledge helped her to accept the fact that he hadn't written to her.

"The recession's biting everywhere," he was explaining. "Not much work about for us musicians. Not too much work about for anybody." It was why he'd accepted this job. And why, if things went well, he envisaged staying on for a while to search for a more permanent contract.

She was beginning to get a sense of her father's plight. There's always another side to the problem, she told herself. It's tough to write and pretend things are great when they're not and you're feeling blue.

So when her dad discovered that the valve on his trumpet had cracked and Pavel reassured him that the finest music shop in Poland was right there in Gdansk, Molly was eager to help. She offered to take the trumpet to the music shop and wait there while the piece was replaced.

Her dad was more than grateful. "But will you find your way?" was his concern.

Radek and Bartosz, always in search of a plausible excuse to offload the responsibility of looking after their baby sister, volunteered to accompany her.

"Make sure they do it on the spot, Moll. I need it for this evening," her father reminded her for the umpteenth time as the trio set off.

Radek said that while they were waiting for the trumpet to be mended he would introduce Molly to the best pinball café in town. Bartosz ribbed his brother about that. "There's only *one* pinball machine in this city. It arrived a couple of months ago from the States. You have to queue to use it."

The lifestyle which Molly had always taken for granted, which included many very ordinary privileges such as being able to find a café with a pinball machine if you wanted one, had been unavailable to the Polish people during the years of communism. These were the years when the Berlin Wall had isolated everybody in Eastern Europe from the West, years when listening to certain pop music might be judged as an act against the state, when there was nowhere to buy a hamburger if you wanted one, when cinema was censored – when everybody had employment...

Molly swung her dad's trumpet case as she strolled, taking in the amazing sights and considering all these differences. She realized how lucky she was to be seeing the world from a whole other camera angle. Vanessa's American way of life was great, Hollywood was the tops,

but they were only one aspect. As the three of them
wandered through the streets of the old town Molly
asked herself if this meant that Radek and Bartosz were
better or worse off than Jean and Michel, who had
never had jobs, but she did not dare to pose such
questions. And then suddenly Bartosz broke the silence.
"When's your mum arriving?" he asked.

It caught Molly off guard. "My mum?"

"Doesn't she travel with your dad, then?"

How could she own up to them, a fully united family,
that her parents were separated? Anyway, if it all
worked out, in a few days she'd have talked her dad into
coming home.

"Mum's pretty tied up…" she mumbled. "She's got
this new job. High-powered. Keeping her busy all
summer…" It didn't seem to count as a lie.

As they made their way through the streets, chatting
and getting to know one another, Molly noticed a lorry
parked about fifty metres ahead, revving up and
belching out powdery clouds of exhaust fumes. It began
reversing towards a building shrouded in scaffolding.
Clearly the driver hadn't noticed the rickety con-
struction behind him.

"Look out!" she yelled and went pounding off,
beating a path ahead of the two boys.

They quickly caught on to what was happening and
took off after her. But the driver didn't hear Molly's
cries. He rammed his lorry right up against the
scaffolding. Instantly it began to buckle and out of the
chaos of tumbling planks fell a workman. He
plummeted, pot of paint in hand, to the ground and lay
motionless on his back. The pot went rolling across the
pavement.

It looked as though a whole section of the scaffolding
was going to land on top of him, and the lorry was still

moving backwards! Quick as lightning Molly deposited her dad's trumpet on to the pavement and ran to help.

"Stop! Stop! There's a man! You'll kill him!"

Radek went charging towards the cab of the lorry while Bartosz drew abreast of Molly. Together they managed to haul the injured man out of the way of the collapsing planks. He was a little concussed, shocked more than anything else. Thick red paint was spilling everywhere, staining the pavement. Molly hurried to a nearby house in search of water for the injured man.

Once everyone had been reassured that it was paint and not blood and that the decorator was not seriously hurt, Radek suggested that they leave the two men to sort things out between them.

"In any case," Bartosz concurred, "the music shop might close for lunch. It's festival time. We ought to get that trumpet to Mateuz, the owner, as soon as possible, before he shuts up the shop and goes to listen to some jazz."

"Right," agreed Radek.

Molly wasn't listening to a single word of this exchange. She was staring back along the street, panic stricken.

"What's up?" asked Bartosz when he registered the terror on her face.

"Dad's trumpet! Where is it?"

The boys stared at the spot where Molly had dumped it. There was nothing there. *NOTHING*. They ran to and fro, searching everywhere.

The trumpet had gone.

"Oh Lord, it must've been stolen," concluded Bartosz.

"Maybe someone thought it had been dropped and picked it up. Oh God, I hope so, or Dad's going to die when he finds out!" cried Molly.

"If someone has found it they've probably handed it

in at the music shop. It's right around the corner. Everyone knows it," reasoned Radek.

"Or we could go to the police," suggested Bartosz.

"It's not stolen, it's lost," argued Radek.

"Lost and Found is right across town. The police are closer," said Bartosz.

Molly felt scared about going to the police, especially in a strange country. She felt sure that if she did her dad would find out what had happened.

"Mateuz's music shop is the obvious place," continued Radek. "I mean, it's where I'd go if I found a trumpet case lying on the ground. Why don't we try it?"

"Which way?"

Radek pointed out a lane. Before anyone could draw breath Molly was off, haring along in a panic.

"Jeez, I hope it's there," confided Radek to his brother.

When they arrived at the shop it was closed. The sign on the door read: "*I shall be closing at lunchtime each day during the festival. In an emergency contact me at the Festival Café.*" It was signed *Mateuz*.

Molly stared hopelessly through the window.

"I can't see it," she said to herself more than to the others. Her face was pressed against the glass.

How could she have been so dumb as to have lost her dad's trumpet? It was the most precious possession he owned, and his sole means of making a living! *First I get myself expelled and then I lose Dad's trumpet!*

"Molly, are you listening to me? I think we should go to the police. There are a lot of thieves about these days," counselled Bartosz.

"Yeah, and half the police force are as corrupt as any of them! Let's try the Festival Café first. With luck Mateuz'll be there. He probably has the trumpet with him. Maybe, as he was closing, somebody handed it in to him. Not everyone's dishonest, brother."

"Sounds logical," said Molly. "Let's go."

They walked back across town, skirting the docks, until they reached the waterside coffee bar known as the Festival Café.

Everyone except for Molly appeared to be in a party mood. Music was playing, the atmosphere was noisy and animated, a holiday spirit pervaded. The sun was shining, making the oil-slicked water glisten with the colours of the rainbow. Molly and her two new pals zigzagged in and out of the jumble of crowded tables searching for Mateuz, but he didn't appear to be there.

"You two keep looking. I'll go inside and see if he's at the bar." Bartosz headed off, leaving Radek and Molly to continue their search.

"It's the only thing that makes my dad angry," said Radek as they moved to and fro. "Touch his saxophone and he hits the roof. If I were you I wouldn't go home."

"Radek, *please* don't make me feel worse."

Then Molly caught sight of her dad. He was sitting at a table a few metres in front of her with Pavel. The pair of them were surrounded by a group of people, laughing and chattering animatedly.

At that same moment Bartosz came out of the café. Pavel spotted his son and began waving, beckoning him over. Bartosz smiled and approached the table.

"I have to stop Bartosz saying anything to Dad before I do!" Molly darted towards the table, reaching it just seconds after Bartosz. Luckily for her, Bartosz appeared to know everyone. This waylaid him. He paused, and then became engrossed in conversation with a beautiful dark-haired woman.

All of this gave Molly the opportunity to reach her dad first. It suddenly crossed her mind that *if* Mateuz had been given the trumpet case and *if* he had opened it and found Peter's name engraved on the trumpet, then he might have already returned it to Peter. This would mean that her dad would know she had lost it.

He saw her hovering uncertainly. Assuming that her reticence was born of shyness he waved her over.

Judging by his good humour, he knew nothing. Was this worse or better? Certainly it meant that she would have to be the one to break the news...

"Molly!"

She approached tentatively, her heart beating fast. "Hi, Dad!"

"How about this place? Pretty special, eh? There are some great musicians here. And you know what?"

"What?"

"It's as I hoped. If this series of concerts goes well, there's permanent work for me here. What's the news about the cracked valve? Is it mended?"

Molly took a deep breath. "I haven't got the trumpet, Dad."

"But it'll be ready for tonight?" He was frowning, not angrily but not understanding her drift.

She felt weak and miserable, plucking up the courage to tell him. "It's gone, Dad."

"Gone? What do you mean, gone?"

"There was a lorry. I was trying to save someone's —"

"My trumpet, Molly! Where is it?"

"I put it down in the street and rushed to save this bloke from —"

"You left my trumpet in the street?"

"Radek says that Pavel will get Mateuz to lend you one for tonight. Just until it turns up again. It's bound to —"

"*You left my trumpet in the street?*"

Pavel telephoned the police, but no musical instrument

had been handed in. He organized the temporary loan of another trumpet for his friend.

They were playing that evening at the Vistula Blues Club. It was a regular date of Pavel's and the ideal spot for Peter to be introduced to the local music scene. Peter's first official concert was scheduled for the following evening: a fancy-dress carnival organized by the city of Gdansk. It was tipped to be the highlight of the festival. All the international musicians currently visiting the city would be playing there.

Molly and the two boys, Radek and Bartosz, accompanied them to the Vistula Blues Club. Peter said no more about the loss of his trumpet, but Molly translated his silence as reproach.

She didn't attempt to explain how bad she felt. Nothing, except the trumpet's return, could make things right.

It was a while since she'd heard her dad performing. In spite of everything he played well, but not to the standard she knew him capable of.

"He's a pretty cool musician, your dad," said Radek when Peter had finished his spot.

Molly nodded.

It was great to hear the reception he attracted, both from the audience and from the other musicians. But she saw the disappointment on his face. He prided himself on his ability and this was less than his best. The audience applauded and Peter took his bow, left the stage and returned to the table where Molly and the boys were seated.

All the dreams she had been harbouring to help him find work, to make him happy, to bring her folks back together again – she'd blown it. What now?

"That's quite a long face you're wearing, Molly."

It took Molly by surprise when the young dark-haired

woman seated next to her spoke. The woman laughed. "I'm Kasia. I sing with Pavel's group."

Molly had vaguely noticed Bartosz speaking to her earlier at the Festival Café.

"I suppose your father's upset with you about his trumpet?"

"He's pretty mad, but I don't blame him. Tomorrow's carnival is a big night for him. You know, for getting work. Playing with another instrument isn't the same."

"Would you like me to help you find it?"

Molly turned to look at the woman more closely. Kasia was smiling warmly. Molly realized that she was beautiful.

"Thanks, but we've looked everywhere. And Pavel's already called the police."

"Has anyone thought of the Russian Market?"

Molly didn't understand. "Russian Market?"

"Keep your voice low. I'll take you in the morning."

Nine

Molly agreed to say nothing about where she and Kasia were heading. It was to be their secret.

They met at a crossroads a kilometre or so from where the Kowalski family lived and from there they set off together, walking briskly, until they reached the outskirts of the city.

The "Market" was a sprawling expanse of wasteland, rubbled and neglected. On this site traders had gathered and an open-air market of sorts was evolving. Every conceivable item could be bought there. For the most part the wares appeared to be secondhand.

"Why is it called 'Russian Market'?" asked Molly as they wandered amongst the strangers, eyeing the goods on display.

"The first to set up trade were Russians. Ordinary people. Since the borders between Poland, Russia and the West have opened up, thousands of starving Russians have crossed the frontiers. They are trying to sell their possessions, hoping to make a little money to take back to their families.

"Recently this site, this 'Russian Market', has become known to the more orthodox traders and buyers as a place to find a bargain, to buy anything, to sell anything. No licence required. So thieves mingle with the poor folk and sell off stolen goods at irresistible prices. Items change hands swiftly. This city of Gdansk is a port, Molly. From here goods can be smuggled to anywhere in the world. Stolen goods are purchased and delivered to ships bound for the West the same evening."

Molly's eyes were wide with the sense of a real-life adventure. She was intrigued. "Is it dangerous?" she asked.

"It can be. Fights break out from time to time. Occasionally one hears or reads of a stabbing or a murder. Amongst rogues there is little honour."

Did such places exist in London or Paris? Molly had no way of knowing. This was film stuff, stories, hardly real life. Leastways, not the real life she inhabited. It thrilled her to think that she was in a world so alien to her own. A smile crossed her face when she considered what her mum would say if she knew where her daughter was at this minute, discovering a frontier land as crooked and potentially dangerous as the Wild West must once have been. She wanted to hug Kasia for bringing her here, for befriending her and showing her such a slice of life.

"Is that why you wanted our visit here to be kept secret?"

Kasia considered the question. "I think most importantly I did not want to raise your father's hopes, only to dash them again if his trumpet is not here."

Molly felt heavy at the reminder of her dad's trumpet. For a while she had almost forgotten it. She glanced up and down the lines of people, scanning the goods on offer. There was no sign of a trumpet.

A woman standing a few metres away from them, with flushed plump cheeks and hair scraped back into a tight bun, held out a fist towards Molly. Molly took a step closer to see what she was holding. The woman unfolded her fingers and there, in the palm of her podgy, work-scuffed hand, was a duckling, fluffy and trembling. The woman pushed her hand once more towards Molly, signalling her to accept the newborn creature. Molly shook her head uncertainly. She would have liked to touch the tiny bird, to cradle and stroke it, but she feared that if she did the woman might assume she wanted to buy it and she had no desire to disappoint her.

"I'm looking for a trumpet," said Kasia to the woman. "Top quality. Do you know of anyone who might be selling one?"

The woman considered the question and then pointed them in the direction of another trader. His stall was somewhere in the middle of the market, in an area they had not yet investigated. "Look out for Grygor. He's a thin fellow with a silver beard. He'll help you."

Kasia said her thanks and was gone, moving determinedly, in search of the man known as Grygor.

Grygor's display, laid out on the ground on rough blankets and wooden boxes of many differing heights, included an assortment of musical instruments alongside a modest collection of antique jewellery – golden bracelets, white pearls as dazzling as teeth, chunky ruby and emerald bejewelled necklaces. But there was no trumpet. Kasia paced up and down slowly past the goods on offer. Out of some unexplained instinct, Molly kept her distance. She watched the business-like approach of Kasia who, having assured herself that no trumpet was anywhere to be seen, demanded of Grygor the same question she had put to the woman with the duckling.

Grygor studied Kasia and she returned his scrutiny with a broad, easy smile. He was weighing her up, deciding whether or not to help her. Molly crept closer, fearing to miss any of the exchange. The stranger's eyes were hooded, lizard-like, and his manner was guarded. He looked mean, meaner than Michel and Jean's polystyrene gangsters. *Maybe Grygor was a real crook!*

Molly thought Kasia was brilliant, like no one she had ever met before. So beautiful, yet tough and resilient. Clearly this man did not faze her, whatever he might be.

Molly watched on, sketching thriller films in her head, inspired by all that Kasia had told her about this place and by everything she was observing and inventing.

The man had still not responded to Kasia's question. Kasia remained calm, smiling patiently, keeping her wits about her.

"You have a fine display here," she continued, coaxing him now with praise.

"I specialize in collectors' pieces. Valuable stuff." His voice was gruff, mistrusting.

"But not a trumpet. Ah, well, more's the pity. Thank you for your help. Good day," and Kasia strode boldly away.

Molly was startled because she felt certain that the man was holding out on them. And she had been convinced that Kasia had seen that in his eyes. Was she testing him?

And then, as though in answer to Molly's silent question, the man called Kasia back. "Curiously, I came across one this very morning. Damned good one, too. Made in England."

In England!

Molly's heart began to race. It had to be her dad's trumpet. She moved still closer, drawing alongside Kasia. With the barest brush of her hand against Molly's thigh, Kasia warned her to keep quiet. *Give nothing away*, the touch seemed to signal. Molly took a deep, calming breath.

"May I see it, please?" Kasia's voice was smooth, almost seductive.

Grygor gave her another of his appraising looks, then turned to a battered old suitcase hidden under a blanket on the ground. He bent down and flicked the rusty clasps.

There, inside, was the trumpet case.

Molly gasped with a mixture of relief and amazement. She felt a slight nudge on her thigh. It was Kasia warning her to keep calm. Grygor opened up the case and revealed Peter's trumpet.

"That's it!" cried Molly.

Kasia's voice was cool and controlled. "What's your feeling about this one, Molly?" she said as she took hold of the instrument. "Do you think my husband would like this one?"

Only for a split second was Molly confused. Once she'd cottoned on, she nodded. "Yeah, he'll think it's *exactly the one*."

Kasia held the trumpet skywards, a musician's pose, then sideways, examining it, noting the initials P G engraved in its golden metal. "Yes, I feel sure this is the one. We will take it, if the price is reasonable."

"*You're not going to pay for it?*" The question whooshed out of Molly's mouth before she could swallow it back.

Kasia ignored the slip, but Grygor eyed her with suspicion. His gaze made Molly squirm, as though she were the guilty one.

"How much did you say?" asked Kasia, still play-acting.

"Eight million zlotys. Five hundred dollars. A bargain."

"That's daylight robbery!"

"It does seem a little expensive," cajoled Kasia. "What would you say to one million?"

Grygor's eyes grew smaller and colder and his voice more flinty. "You're wasting my time." He leant forward to snatch back the trumpet, but Kasia skipped backwards beyond his reach. Now old Grygor knew for sure that something was up. He lurched towards Kasia, grabbed the trumpet and stuffed it greedily back into its case. They'd lost it for a second time!

When his back was turned Molly leaned towards her new friend. "I'm going for the police," she whispered.

Kasia shook her head.

"Why not? Why don't we just report him? He'll be arrested and we can take it. It's Dad's!"

"Go on, get away from here!" Grygor hissed at them when he realized they were still there.

"That's my dad's trumpet! Stolen yesterday! You have no right to keep it!"

"Molly!"

Molly paid no heed to Kasia's warning. She manoeuvred her way past the boxes, intent on reaching the suitcase. The silver-haired fellow intervened by grabbing at her arm. "If you don't get away from here right this minute, there'll be serious trouble. Now scram!"

"We would like to buy the trumpet," said Kasia.

"No, we wouldn't! It's already ours. It belongs to my dad. I'm going for the police!" cried Molly, pulling herself free.

Heads were turning. People were staring, curious to know what the rumpus was about. One scrawny, furtive-looking man further along the line of traders slipped his few bits of jewellery into a paper bag and scuttled away. The word "police" had obviously rung a warning bell.

"The catches on the case are solid silver. You keep that and we take... we *buy* the trumpet. I think one million zlotys was the price we had settled on." Kasia was digging in her purse in search of the necessary money. Grygor did not respond, but neither did he tell them to get lost again. He was considering the offer.

Kasia, cash in hand, lifted her head and held the money firmly between her fingers. "Please unpack the trumpet. We need to take it *now*."

He was thinking, weighing things up.

"I learnt from one of your fellow traders that you have been charged with handling stolen goods at least once before. If I send my young friend here for the police..."

He flinched visibly.

He was a crook!

"Another offence might put you in jail. Here is the one million zlotys."

Grygor accepted the notes without a word. Grudgingly he retrieved the trumpet and case from their hiding place. "Here, take it, case 'n' all, and get out of my sight!"

Once they were clear of the Russian Market, out of danger and safely en route for the old town, Kasia handed the dark blue case over to Molly.

"Here," she said. "When your father sees you with this, it will make him very happy."

"Aren't you coming with me?"

"No, you return it to him."

"But why? Dad will want to thank you."

"I would prefer that he believes you retrieved it from somewhere by yourself. The market, our adventure there together, will remain our secret."

Molly was puzzled. "I don't understand."

Kasia laughed. "He's your father. You are the one who needs to make things up with him."

"But I'll never be able to pay you back."

"It's a present from one new friend to another."

Molly was speechless. Kasia's kindness was overwhelming. "Thanks! You're a real pal."

"He's a talented man, Molly, and from all that he has told me his daughter is equally gifted."

Molly, clutching the trumpet, determined that it wouldn't leave her sight even for a second until it was back in her dad's hands, stopped walking. "Dad talked to you about me?"

"Yes. Does that upset you?"

"Of course not. But when?"

"Outside the Festival Café yesterday afternoon. He told me—"

"Did he mention Mum?"

For the first time, Kasia appeared reticent. She paused, apparently to consider Molly's question. "He loves you very much and he's very proud of you, Molly. That's what counts."

"Yeah?" Molly felt warm and glowing. It never occurred to her that her dad might be proud of her.

And then she remembered that he still didn't know she'd been expelled.

"I'd better get this back to him. He'll want to rehearse before this evening. But why did you pay for it instead of informing the police?"

"If the police had become involved they would have kept the trumpet as evidence against old Grygor, at least until after he'd been charged. Peter – your father's – need was too urgent. He would never have had it returned to him for a concert this evening. Better this way. I'll see you at the carnival tonight." And with that Kasia leant forward, kissed Molly on the cheek and was on her way, calling as an afterthought, "Oh, by the way, did you notice that the valve has been fixed?"

Molly hadn't noticed. She shook her head, watched Kasia's departing back for an instant and then, triumphant in the knowledge that nothing in the world would please her dad more than the sight of his trumpet, she ran full pelt through the streets of old Gdansk.

She thought of what her dad had said to Kasia. He was proud of her. Things would be brilliant between them from now on, even once she'd explained about college.

It wasn't the end of the world. She could go to another school, find somewhere right in the heart of Paris. And before too long her dad would come back home, she was certain. They would be together again as a family. That was what counted. Life was going to be better than ever before.

Molly felt confident.

Ten

When Molly handed her dad his trumpet he said, "With a bit of luck, my girl, you'll be back here for Christmas!" His delight was evident.

"So you'll stay, then?"

"Work is work, Molly. If Gdansk is where it's offered, then this is where I'll be."

The idea didn't upset Molly. She held on tightly to her dream of bringing her parents back together. They had left England for her father's work and they could as easily live in Poland as France, at least for a time. Maybe it would mean her going away to another boarding school, but she could handle it now. She could handle anything so long as they were a family.

The most pressing step was to reunite her mum and dad. And for that they needed to be in the same town. So, while Peter and Pavel rehearsed and while Radek and Bartosz prepared their fancy dress costumes for the carnival, Molly took off for the post office and put in a call to her mum.

Still Alice's voice and the same recorded message. Why wasn't she answering the phone? If she'd gone away, where could she be? Could she have returned to England in search of Peter? That wasn't very likely. Alice had told Molly that she'd been seeing Peter in Paris. Molly found it very curious. She was on the point of hanging up when the tone sounded. If she wanted to leave a message, now was her moment to do it.

"Mum, listen, Dad and me... we're still in Poland. I'm posting you a letter right now, with our address. Dad's got heaps of work here. He says *you've got to come and join us.* He misses you like crazy. We both do."

She replaced the receiver and scribbled a rough note giving Pavel's address, adding as an afterthought in big capitals: DON'T BOTHER TO ANSWER. JUST GET HERE. See ya soon. Love, Moll.

When Alice received the letter she'd be bound to get on the next plane. Molly bought a stamp and posted it. She should have done this sooner. Then she made her way back to the Kowalski's.

She had to tell her dad about being expelled before her mum did. If he was going to be mad, better to get it over with. Then, once Alice was there, they could move on to the business of being a family again.

If all goes well at the carnival, Molly was thinking as she ran back home, Dad will be in a fantastic mood. After his show, when he's on a real high, that's the moment to drop the bombshell. He'll be too happy to raise a storm. And by the time Mum arrives in Gdansk the whole business will have blown over and Dad won't let Mum be angry with me.

Perfect. Molly had settled it in her mind.

The choice of fancy dress costumes had been Molly's idea. Bartosz had suggested the Three Musketeers, but Molly had said they'd be better off picking something modern. "Easier to put together," she'd explained. Her experience with the girls in the dorm had taught her that much.

"What, then?"

"Pencil moustache, raincoat, hat, water pistol."

"What are we meant to be?" Radek was thinking about it. Bartosz didn't have a clue.

"TV detectives."

"So simple!"

"And brilliant, Molly."

They painted on the moustaches with black felt-tip pens and swiped macs from the adults. Molly borrowed her dad's. She knew he wouldn't object. They'd bought the water pistols and the hats were on loan from some pal of Radek's. Molly had managed to acquire a trilby, the real McCoy. Perched on her mass of wild blonde hair, it was a showstopper!

She fancied herself as Harpo Marx.

Their entrance into the living room, where the Kowalski family and Peter had already mustered, caused an explosion of applause.

"Hey, you've pinched my raincoat!" Her dad was laughing as he said it. He loved it when she came up with neat ideas. And tonight he was in such a good humour, holding on to his trumpet and looking suave in his evening suit (cooler than Eric Clapton!). It was clear that nothing was going to rile him.

They set off from the house together, Pavel and Anya (Radek and Bartosz's fat mum), Radek and Bartosz, Molly and her dad. Grandma Kowalski stayed at home to look after the little ones. In any case, she was too deaf to appreciate music. The adults were walking side by side, a few steps ahead of Molly and the boys, who were lagging behind, telling silly jokes.

"What's green, covered in teeth marks and wears a bowler hat?"

"Spearmint gum going to the office!"

They hooted with laughter. It wasn't even funny. Their reaction was an expression of the loony mood they were in. Molly felt crazily lighthearted. She'd left the message for her mum and posted their address. *Her mum was on her way.* She could feel her problems slipping gently away and life resolving itself. It was brilliant to see her dad all dressed up, swinging it in his embroidered waistcoat. He was over-the-moon happy too.

Passing through the old town, they turned into the lane where Molly had seen the brooch. The others kept walking while she paused outside the shop. It was still there in the centre of the display – *her* brooch. The window was illuminated by red spotlights. The silver butterfly wings glinted in the light and the amber body looked rich and heavy, like runny honey. It would be great to offer it as a welcome gift to her mum.

Radek called to her to get a move on.

"Coming!" But Molly hesitated.

If the shop was open she'd slip in and ask the price. She had very little money, but asking made the dream feel possible.

The shop was closed.

After one last glance she took off at a pace, clutching tightly to her trilby so that it wouldn't blow away.

She'd mention the brooch to her dad later. Not now. Now she wasn't even going to tell him that Mum was coming. Let it be a huge surprise.

The carnival gig was held on an old sailing ship in the harbour – a wooden clipper with tall masts covered in plastic bunting. The musicians were grouped towards the stern and the dancing and chairs took up the rest of the deck.

The ticket-collector was waiting by the gangplank, dressed as one of the Addams family. Molly's dad had hers, but Lurch let her on board anyway when she explained that she was the trumpet player's daughter.

She made her way through the partying people in search of her crowd as the boat swayed with the waves. Then she spotted Kasia standing with some people near the makeshift bandstand. She was looking amazing. Her long black hair was shining and she was dressed in a black slinky frock, looking like the most edible liquorice in the world.

Molly thought of the brooch. Kasia could negotiate a price which would make it affordable. Kasia could do *anything*. Molly watched her chatting and laughing with the group around her. She was even more beautiful than Vanessa. Must be brilliant to look like that. She was a cool singer, too. Molly had heard her after they'd talked at the Vistula Blues Club.

She caught sight of Radek and Bartosz. They were carrying their water pistols, behaving as though they were casing the joint. She negotiated a path towards them. They hadn't spotted her, so she crept up on them from behind, stuck her pistol in Radek's back and said, "Git 'em up, mister!"

Both boys swung round, then laughed. "Where've you been?"

"Looking at a welcome present for my mum."

"You said she wasn't coming."

"She's changed her mind." It seemed unnecessary to go into details. At that moment Pavel and Peter climbed up on to the stage. "Hey, look!"

They pushed through to the front of the crowd, better to see and hear their dads make music.

Molly knew her father was having a brilliant time. He was a huge success. His sets had gone a bomb. Everyone said so.

Now she was trying not to feel jealous. She really liked Kasia... but she and Peter had been dancing together ever since they'd finished on the stage.

It was clear that they'd really enjoyed playing together, Kasia and Molly's dad and Pavel. That was fine. Molly was proud of that. Proud, too, of the reception her dad had been given, especially after his solos. She'd known by the quiet smile in his eyes that he felt he'd played his best.

All of that was no problem. It was what was happening now that was unsettling her. It wasn't even anything she could put her finger on. Just all the dancing.

She'd planned to sit with him and tell him outright, "Listen, Dad, I've been expelled." Even without this sudden interest in Kasia it wouldn't have been easy. Holding a conversation above the racket would have been a struggle. The carnival had grown rowdy. But she might at least have been able to pave the way, lead up to it, tell him in bits if necessary, but definitely tell him. He was in such a good mood. The evening was going so well.

She couldn't let this opportunity slip by. She might not get this chance again.

And now here she was sitting in a corner, watching Kasia and her dad whirl about the floor together, like they couldn't see anyone else.

Even Pavel was ready to go home. Bartosz was half asleep and Radek kept scratching at his face, smudging his moustache and making the tip of his nose black. He looked like a dopey rabbit.

There was no way she was going to get her dad's ear tonight.

Maybe later, when she was in bed, before he went to clean his teeth. Kasia wouldn't be there then...

The trouble was, she didn't feel like telling him now. She had to be in the right frame of mind. Now she was just tired and fed up, and mad at Kasia for hogging her dad's attention, even though she really liked her.

Her father didn't leave with her. He stayed on and told her he'd see her later. Kasia gave her a warm goodnight hug, knocking Molly's trilby off her head, but she was past caring. She whispered in her ear, "Your father was splendid. We helped make his evening, didn't we?"

Pavel walked back with them and Molly was fast asleep before her dad got in.

He must have got up and gone out early because when she woke his bed was made. She had no idea where he'd disappeared to. No one else seemed to know either. When she enquired they didn't even look at her. They smiled reassuringly and told her not to fret, that he'd be back soon.

She wasn't fretting. She just didn't know where he was. She thought she must be feeling what her mum used to feel when he didn't come home after his gigs.

SHOOT! Maybe he hadn't come back last night either.

When she helped Anya, Radek's mum, to lay the table for lunch, Molly asked her. "Dad came back last night, didn't he?"

"You were asleep and didn't hear him. Now stop fussing."

Everyone was hedging.

She tried reading and listening to her Walkman. It didn't work, nor did writing in her notebook, so she decided to go out for a bit.

She vaguely thought of heading for the Festival Café. Maybe her dad was there. She took her Walkman with her and stuffed a few cassettes into her body purse. If she didn't find him she could sit down at the harbour, watch the boats and listen to some sounds.

Without really thinking about it she found herself back in the heart of the old town, wandering along the jewellery shop lane. It wasn't lunchtime yet. The shop was bound to be open.

The bell on the door jangled as Molly entered. Inside it smelt musky. It was too silent, as though someone was watching her.

Three glass cabinets were laid out with amber and silver pieces. There wasn't much, but it was nicely arranged, with huge loopy earrings and long dangly ones, some hanging from wire stalks, so that the display looked layered. It was elegant.

Molly scanned the cabinets. There was no sign of the butterfly brooch. She felt a cold panic at the idea that it might have been sold. She looked about her. At the back of the shop was a beaded curtain, probably leading to the shopkeeper's home.

"Hello?"

No one answered. No one came to serve her. She coughed loudly and heard the shuffle of feet.

From beyond the swing of the beaded curtain an old man appeared, wearing moon-shaped spectacles perched on the tip of his nose. He peered at Molly over the top of the glasses, just like Madame Savère always did. His look was one of mistrust. "Yes?" he said.

"I want to know how much a brooch costs."

"Each has a different price."

"The butterfly one." Molly refused to let his manner faze her. "It was in the window. Now it's gone."

"Ah, the laced silver. A very special piece." His face lit up at the recollection of the brooch. "Someone has asked me to keep it aside for them."

"It's sold?"

"He'll return later."

"Don't sell it! Please don't!"

And she was gone. It was irrational – she hadn't even found out the price. But she didn't think of that; she thought only of buying the brooch before the customer returned.

Neither did she stop to consider whether the Russian Market would be operating that day. Fortunately it was.

She didn't have a clue where to begin. One trader was probably as good as any other, so she headed for the woman with the fluffy birds.

"Hi. I want to sell my Walkman." She showed the Walkman. The woman stared as though she'd never set eyes on Molly before. "And my cassettes." Silence. "They're not stolen, honest. I just need cash."

"Two hundred and forty thousand zlotys."

Without Kasia there to help her Molly didn't have a clue how much this was. "How much is that in real money?" she asked weakly.

The woman didn't understand Molly's question. "Two hundred and forty thousand zlotys," she repeated.

"I'll take it."

When Molly returned to the shop, the butterfly brooch had been sold.

When she got back to the house, Radek told her that she'd sold her Walkman for about fourteen dollars, or six pounds fifty.

The picnic was her dad's idea, but it was Bartosz who suggested the castle at Marlbork.

Everyone was in high spirits – laying out the cloth, talking over sandwiches, spraying fizzy drinks.

No one paid any attention when Kasia turned up, except Molly, and her dad, who'd evidently been the one to invite her. Instead of feeling pleased, Molly felt a great gloom descend upon her. Within seconds Peter was taking photos of Kasia and immediately afterwards the two of them disappeared inside the castle.

Under the pretext of visiting the museum with Radek and Bartosz, Molly followed them. While the boys strolled through corridors of armour, she slid off in search of her dad and Kasia.

Eventually she caught sight of them. She was standing on a turret, leaning out, scanning the people some distance below. Dozens of them were wandering about like ants in an inner courtyard. Kasia and Molly's dad had left the courtyard and were crossing a narrow bridge. Kasia was a few steps ahead of him. Laughing, she stopped and turned back. Peter drew close to her.

In spite of leaning right out over the castle wall and balancing on her tummy it was difficult for Molly to see exactly what was going on. Her dad was taking something out of his pocket. It was small, maybe a coin. She couldn't make out what it was. He held it towards Kasia and Kasia's face lit up. Molly saw that quite definitely.

Kasia touched Peter's outstretched hand and he stepped closer. Molly was feeling panicky about what she was seeing. He was touching Kasia, fiddling with her clothes.

He was pinning a *brooch* on to her blouse. It was glinting in the sunlight. Molly's heart began to race.

No! She turned and descended stone steps, a spiral stairway, clomping and leaping. She had to be near them. *She had to see*.

Molly landed in the courtyard as Kasia was about to embrace Peter. She flung open her arms but in so doing knocked her camera from the bridge into a grass ditch beneath them. She made a grab for it, but failed to catch it. Peter disappeared, intent on retrieving the camera. Kasia waited on the bridge.

She was alone when Molly drew up, puffing and frantic. She smiled and Molly stared at her – at the blouse and the butterfly brooch.

"That's not for you!"

"Sorry?" Kasia's confusion was covered by Peter's return.

"It's not broken!" he shouted and then, when he saw his daughter, he added, "Hello there, Molly!"

Molly rounded on him in fury, tears in her eyes. "What's she doing with the brooch?"

"Molly... " Her father took a step towards her.

"It's for Mum!"

"It isn't—"

"You said we might buy it. And she's coming. Any day now she'll be here!"

"No..."

"It's a surprise!"

Peter spoke softly and calmly, resting a hand on Molly's shoulder. "Molly, listen to me... she's not coming."

"Yes she is. I sent her a card, told her about your job—"

"Molly, your mum and I—"

"When you found work, she said... it would all be good again..."

"Molly, we're divorced."

"*Div*—"

Stunned. Skittled. Like in a Western, punched in the guts. Molly looked from one to the other. The two adults stared down at her, gauging how she was taking it. Allies. It was obvious: Kasia knew. She'd said, "Your dad told me things" at the Festival Café. Divorced!

Everyone knew except her. Betrayed by her own dad!

She had to get away. Turning, Molly fled, angry tears burning her face and the wind slicing her cheeks as she ran.

Divorced!

She was packing her stuff when she heard him coming up the stairs calling her name. Quick as a flash she kicked her backpack under the bed and threw herself on to the mattress, face to the wall. The door opened. She knew without even looking that he was mad as hell.

But so was she.

"We've been looking everywhere for you."

She didn't respond.

"You're hurt, I understand. But that doesn't give you the right to lose your temper and charge off in a sulk."

She still didn't turn around; she wasn't letting him off the hook.

"You wanted to come with me, you insisted on coming—"

"Why didn't you just tell me?" she wailed, the anger no longer able to contain the depth of her pain.

"Your mother and I didn't want to spoil your chances at college. She was planning to tell you in the holidays, face to face. Then you turned up in Paris and begged to come with me. There was no opportunity."

"You could have told me on the plane! You have no right to keep things from me!"

"You were expelled. Have you mentioned it? No. Now stop hollering and listen to me." He perched beside her on the bed and wheeled her body round so that she was facing him.

Molly dropped her gaze.

"Look at me."

He was holding her by the shoulders. She longed for

him to close his arms tightly around her and make her feel safe, put the pieces of her shattered world back into a tight warm ball. She looked up into his eyes.

"Listen, sweetheart, sometimes life is painful, but you've got to learn to let go. It's the only way to keep people."

"Let go of what?"

"Me, for a start."

"You're my dad!"

"And I'll always be your dad. That won't change. You have your mother and you have me. We both love you. But our marriage is the past, Molly. We don't want to spend our lives together any more."

"What about me?"

"I told you we both love you. We just won't be doing it alongside one another any more."

Molly closed her eyes. The loss of her father. It was too much to bear. "What about Kasia? Do you love her too?"

"It's too soon to know those things, love."

She thought her heart would burst.

"The show goes on, Molly."

That night, while her father was sleeping Molly slid her backpack from under the bed and left the house. On the pillow, alongside his sleeping face, she left a note.

It read:

Dad, I can't stay any longer. If you speak to Mum tell her I'm safe and I'll see her soon. I love you. Molly.

Eleven

With the fourteen dollars cash from the sale of her Walkman, Molly bought a train ticket. This took her right across Poland to visit Daniela, who lived on the far-flung outskirts of the Polish and Russian border. (No wonder Molly thought Dan sounded like a Russian spy in a James Bond movie!) She was there an entire week before Dan's grandfather discovered that she'd run away, and in that time she met Dan's brother Dominik, the most *gorgeous* guy she'd ever set eyes on, and fell swoony tongue-tied in love with him.

It happened like this... No wait! Molly, on the run, that's a whole other story...

When the news was out that Molly had run away, Dan's grandfather talked to her mum in Paris and four days later Molly was on a plane back home.

Alice was pretty mad at Molly for running away. At least Molly guessed she must be. Although Alice said very little. Except, "Get your travel bag cleaned out please, Molly. I'm taking you away."

"Taking me away?"

"I want no argument, please.'

Molly found herself sitting in a coach alongside her mum, heading for the south of France. She interpreted her mother's silence as her mum being super mad, meaning that she was so angry she couldn't bring herself to speak.

Molly had been expelled. Molly had gone running. Everyone had been looking for her.

Shoot!

She decided to keep her head down, say little and hope that the storm would pass without too much damage.

The trip her mother had organized for them was to an island off the Mediterranean coast. Albert, the restauranteur Alice had worked for in Paris, the fat guy who had accompanied her to the benefit night, had sold his bistro in Belleville and bought a hotel on the island. In other words, if Molly had got things right, they were on their way to visit Albert!

Why they were going to spend their holidays at Albert's place, Molly had no idea. Nor did she enquire. She didn't feel that the current state of affairs between her mother and herself allowed for too many questions. She was playing it safe. When her mother had told her to pack her bags and not argue, she had packed her bags and made no objections.

Perhaps Albert had offered them a deal on the price of the rooms.

They arrived at the old port in Cannes, the embarkation point for the ferry to the island. Albert wasn't there to meet them, so they had to lug their bags by themselves from the coach station to the ferry booking office. It seemed to take forever, Molly's mother was travelling with so many suitcases.

Alice's mood had changed and she was suddenly very bright and breezy. Molly knew her mother did that when she was nervous or hiding something. Alice charged Molly with keeping an eye on the luggage while she went in search of ferry tickets.

"Anyone'd think you're planning to stay over there, you've got so much stuff!" Molly quipped. Alice didn't laugh or even smile, which was the reaction Molly had been expecting. She simply strode off purposefully towards the ticket office. Molly sighed. Clearly, her mum was still mad at her.

As she stood on the quay surrounded by bags, Molly began to think. Alice had cut her hair and was wearing new clothes. She was looking... not dolled up but pretty, really pretty. And on the coach, half an hour or so before they reached Cannes, she'd started fussing with her face, putting on lipstick and perfume. Her mother never behaved like that.

What was there for her to be so nervous about? They were going on holiday.

There was something else, too, which only now dawned on Molly. Alice hadn't lost her temper once, not even when she'd been so angry with her daughter for running off. Nor had she gone spare about Molly's expulsion. All she'd said was, "Done is done, Molly. We'll find an alternative."

Shoot! Molly had been misreading the signals! Her mum wasn't mad at all. She was silent because she was relaxed, easy-going. This was a side of Alice Molly hadn't seen for a while.

Why was she so laid back? Her daughter had been expelled from college and she'd just got divorced. That didn't make people happy, did it?

Easy-going in Paris and nervous now... It couldn't have anything to do with Albert, could it?

Wham! The penny dropped! Her mum was hiding disappointment, nervy because Albert wasn't there.

She couldn't have *fallen* for Albert? It wasn't possible.

Not Albert!

This was the first time it had even entered Molly's head. After all, Albert wasn't someone you'd think you'd need to worry about.

What was it Alice had said during their coach journey? Molly had confided: "… How can I persuade Madame Savère to let me go back to college? I'm missing everyone."

"We'll find somewhere else you'll like, Molly. *Down in the south, perhaps?*"

Shoot!

Now she knew what she was up against Molly's defences would be riding shotgun!

NOT ALBERT, NO WAY.

As it turned out, being grotty to Albert wasn't going to be such a tough mission because, frankly, he wasn't about to win first prize in the Mr Heart-throb stakes. In fact, it was hard to say who Molly was turned off by the most, Albert or his wimpy son Philippe.

Albert was bald and round, and so welcoming Molly just wanted to throw up. When he put his arm around her shoulder, and shook her she thought her bones would unhook! The idea of her mum fancying him was worse than incredible, it was lousy.

Would she have felt the same whoever her mum had picked? Or her dad, for that matter? No. She really liked Kasia. She was hurt and upset with her dad, but that was because her parents hadn't come clean with her about the divorce; they'd let her hope for a reconciliation.

Please, not creepy Albert!

The hotel was a shambles but Molly loved its huge, rambling style. Best of all, there were loads of nooks and crannies to discover and escape to.

And the island was awesome. Five hundred metres up the hill from the hotel was a fortress, a genuine one, so real it looked like the set from an epic movie. She could see it from her bedroom window.

Lawrence of Arabia as the neighbours!

Molly read that the Man in the Iron Mask had been imprisoned there, and Philippe told her that the hotel was haunted by his ghost. Philippe was just a stupid kid and a pain.

As Molly dumped her stuff in her room she noticed something on the table by her bed. Her precious photo – the one of her dad she'd smashed back at school! Her mum must've replaced the glass. Molly was happy to have it back and to know that Alice had gone to such trouble. She went to the kitchen to make herself a sandwhich. She was feeling quite cheerful until Albert walked in and found her there. He was furious. He accused her of making a mess in his kitchen. No kidding, she was hearing straight – *his kitchen*! There were two temporary gas rings in it and a fridge which shimmied like a fan dancer! Underneath his jovial exterior he was a real stickler for tidiness and discipline. Every time he stood up, Molly half expected him to fold away his chair! Alice said it was because he was bringing up his son without a mother, and because he worked as a chef and kitchens were his "arena". But when Molly was alone with her dad he didn't carry on like that. He was cut up when she lost his trumpet, but he didn't hit the roof about unimportant details. He didn't even notice them.

Molly was beginning to regret running away from her dad. She longed to tell him things – how she'd fallen for Dan's brother Dominik and couldn't stop thinking about him; how she was missing her pals from college –

all kinds of stuff she'd never taken the opportunity to
say to him. There was a big empty space in her life. She
was afraid that running away on the spur of the
moment had cut him off from her forever. What he'd
said to her about letting go… she couldn't do it. On the
other hand, she didn't want to end up behaving
possessively like Albert did towards Philippe. How can
you "let go" of your own dad? It wasn't normal.

Later, when Molly strolled up the hill to take a look at
the fortress, she discovered that there was a whole
bunch of kids staying there. She talked to one or two of
them and learnt that they were spending their entire
holidays on the site, attending a summer sailing club.
During lunch Molly asked her mum if she could enrol,
but before Alice could open her mouth, Albert spoke.
He said that if she fancied going out on the sea Philippe
would take her. Philippe went fishing most days and
knew the waters. The previous year, he went on, one of
the youngsters from the sailing club had drowned when
his dinghy had keeled over and sunk.

Molly turned to her mum. She was battling with
herself not to say, *I wasn't asking you, windbag*! or maybe
something even meaner.

"Best to go with Philippe, dear," Alice said.

Molly resented Albert playing the decisionmaker. She
declined his offer politely. Her main reason for wanting
to join the sailing club was so that she could take a look
inside the fortress, currently closed to the public for
renovation work. She was dying to visit the dungeons
and see where the Man in the Iron Mask had been
imprisoned. She had a *brilliant idea* for a musical about
him – heaps of sword fights, rock songs and yummy
love scenes…

She sent a card to Jean and Michel and another to Mr

Beauchamps, offering it as an idea for their next benefit. Mr Beauchamps replied by return of post, informing her that their Chicago evening had raised over thirty thousand francs. More than *three thousand* pounds! Molly was over the moon. She tried to puzzle out approximately how much that might be in Polish zlotys (give or take a million) so that she could send cards to Radek and Bartosz and to Dan and her gorgeous brother Dominik. She sent the cards anyway, giving figures which seemed about accurate.

How she longed to go back to college and be there with the others to share in the success of the California! How she longed to introduce the place to all her new Polish pals, especially Dominik, who was a guitarist like Jean.

Jean sent her a letter. He wrote that while he and Michel had been cleaning away the debris after benefit night at the California, Madame Savère had turned up *to congratulate them.*

"You got the wrong guys, lady. It's Molly Greenfield you should be congratulating, not us. Instead of which you kicked her out!" was what he claimed to have told the headmistress.

Molly was dying to know what Madame Savère's reaction had been, but Jean didn't say.

This news gave Molly the courage to sit down and write a long, heartfelt letter to Madame Savère. She apologized for going against the rules of the college and asked the headmistress to reconsider her expulsion. She explained that she would never have risked the college's reputation if she hadn't been absolutely certain that the evening would turn out to be a rip-roaring success. The last bit wasn't strictly true, but she couldn't think how else to soften Madame Savère's heart. She considered outlining her latest idea, *The Man in the Iron Mask: A*

Hard Rock Extravaganza, but thought this might scare the headmistress off. So eventually she posted the letter with its simple apology and request.

"She's been expelled from school, she ran away from her father, she does as she pleases. She needs discipline and a firm hand." Molly heard Albert's words distinctly. He was discussing her with her mother.

Molly was outside her mum's room. She had been on her way to talk to her and the door had been closed. *She wasn't eavesdropping*. She had heard voices and had paused, waiting. She couldn't just barge in; she had to wait outside. Consequently, she overheard their conversation.

"You can't live your entire life for your daughter, Alice. You must consider your own happiness."

That's what he was saying. Actually, he was talking about his own happiness.

"If she won't settle, if she refuses to accept 'us', we'll find another boarding school for her. I know you don't want to hear this, but her father has been irresponsibly lenient with her. She's a rebel."

And then came her mum's response. "No, I don't think so. I think you're too exacting. Peter encourages her independence."

Good old Dad!

"In any case," continued Alice, "I can't send her away. She's forfeited her scholarship."

"That's not a problem. I'll help with the fees."

Get rid of Molly at any price!

"Please don't let's discuss it any more. I need to talk to Molly first," Alice concluded.

Molly heard Albert's footsteps approaching the door. She scooted along the corridor and closed herself in the linen cupboard until she was certain her mum was alone.

So Albert considered her, Molly, the fly in his greasy ointment!

Shoot!

Albert had left the door of Alice's room ajar. Molly counted to a hundred and then approached and waited, hovering by the door until her mum spied her. Alice was bent over a dressing-table arranging bottles. Half-unpacked cases were all over the place.

Next time her mum nagged her about tidiness Molly would cite the state of this room!

Her mum looked annoyed when she caught sight of her. "Have you been listening?" she snapped.

"I was on my way to talk to you… I heard voices."

"Come in and close the door, please."

Molly obeyed. She watched her mother busying herself at the dressing table, avoiding looking in her direction. "He wants you to live here," Molly said at last.

Her mum took a breath, considering what to say or how to admit it. "Yes, he does."

"Do you want to?"

"I would enjoy helping with the hotel."

"It's not habitable. Not for proper people, anyway."

"When we've redecorated it, silly! It's a pretty island." Alice was looking at her now. There was a softness in her voice.

"Give up our place in Paris?"

"If that's what we d—"

"Move miles away from Dad?"

Alice nudged a bottle so that it slid into line with the others. They were in a row like soldiers. Albert'd like that.

"Is this why you and Dad got divorced?" Molly demanded, struggling against a giant lump in her throat and stupid, shifting emotions. "So you can be with him?"

"No…"

"*Then why*? Why, when we came to France to make it all good again? Why have you and Dad got divorced?" Suddenly the pain and disappointment overwhelmed her. None of this made any sense. What were they doing in this nowhere place? Why, if they couldn't be with her dad, weren't they living in England? Molly began to weep quietly. Life felt such a battle. She didn't know who she could count on any more or when things would ever feel safe again.

Alice stepped away from the dressing table, negotiating suitcases, to reach her daughter.

Standing, head bent, Molly's tears fell. Helplessly, she allowed them to flow.

"Come here." Her mum took her in her arms and squeezed her tight.

"I miss Dad," she wept. "I miss us. It's horrid trying to get used to it."

"Give it time," her mum whispered softly. "It just needs time."

"Do you still think about Dad, too?"

"Of course…"

Molly lifted her head and gazed hard into her mum's face, trying to see what was going on behind it, trying to understand what had caused this mess.

"Please, sweetheart, let's give it a try here. Eh, Molly?"

Molly's heart felt like a freight train had just run through it. She didn't want to refuse. For her mum's sake, she didn't. She hated it when they were prickly with one another, and yet – and yet she couldn't bring herself to smile generously and accept the situation.

"Will you try for me, Molly?"

"If you like…" The words were out, but they felt as dry as twigs in her mouth.

Her plan had been not to give in, not to accept Albert!

"Good girl. We'll all make a super-big effort, eh? And in time, everything will be fine again and we'll look back on this episode and laugh."

Molly had come to her mother's room intending to tell her about the letter she'd posted to Madame Savère. Now she decided to say nothing. For the time being she'd keep things to herself. Bury it inside herself, like a loaded weapon.

Alice and Albert took a trip over to the mainland and Philippe went fishing. There was a circus playing over on the other side of the island, so Molly dug out an old bike from one of the hotel sheds and cycled over to see the show. She loved circuses. She loved the sawdust smell, the enthusiasm and magic, the faded glamour and the way you could see through it all. It was a world from the past, like watching black-and-white and silent movies.

She volunteered to walk the high wire! Before she'd even thought about it she was up there, looking down at the rows of faces staring up at her in horror. It was exhilarating and terrifying falling through the air, plummeting to earth and landing in the safety net. The audience cheered her, the clowns rallied around her. Applause rang in her ears. Afterwards, she bought candy floss and hot dogs and all the disgusting things she fancied and cycled back in the late afternoon sunshine, feeling satisfied with her day.

Her mother had asked her to meet them at the ferry terminal and help load the shopping into Albert's jeep. Molly parked her old bike and waited on the quay. Crowds of tourists and locals came and went. Crates of stuff were being unloaded while boxes were stacked ready to be hauled aboard.

"Ahoy there!" It was Albert waving and smiling.

At first she hadn't recognized them both, they were so weighed down with paint cans and rolls of wallpaper. Albert looked like one of those phoney grinning blokes in a TV commercial.

"Had a good day, sweetheart?"

"Yeah, thanks, Mum."

"What did you do, dear?" Alice was smiling broadly, but there was apprehension in her voice.

"Nothing much." Molly couldn't say why she didn't tell them about the circus, except that she felt a need now to guard things within herself. Secrets were a protective shell.

When all the decorating gear had been packed into the jeep Albert offered her a lift.

"No, thanks; I've got a bike."

"Have you, dear?" said her mother.

"Don't dawdle about down here then, Molly." Albert clambered into his seat. He just couldn't help himself, could he? He turned everything into an order.

The jeep chugged off up the hill.

They had both been in remarkably good humour. They were *making an effort* – the same effort she had promised to make. Everybody was happy because they believed she had accepted their new life. Salvation lay in being invited back to college. She was gunning for it.

It was that or a shoot out at the OK Corral.

She went in search of the bike and set off along the cliffside path to the hotel.

"Molly, did you take Philippe's bike?"

Molly hesitated. "No."

"No?"

"I didn't take it, I borrowed it."

"Did it not occur to you to ask Philippe first?"

She had barely stepped inside the kitchen and there

she was, face to face with Albert looking like flushed thunder, her mother standing awkwardly looking troubled and Philippe at the table, whingeing, "Gone! My bike's gone!"

"No, it hasn't. It's parked against the wall, outside in the lane."

They were at her before she could explain.

"Are you in the habit of helping yourself to other people's possessions?"

"It was in the shed. I needed a bike..." She felt as though she were facing the Inquisition.

"It belongs to me and I needed it!"

"That's not true. You were out fishing in your boat!"

"Molly, you should have asked Philippe first if he needed it." Molly couldn't believe her mother was taking their side.

"He wasn't here! In any case I didn't know it was his. I wouldn't have taken it at all if I'd known there'd be such a fuss! I didn't think —"

"Exactly! You didn't think! And now you have just dumped it outside against the wall where anyone could take it!"

Molly stared at Albert. He was really enjoying himself, laying into her like this. What had happened to all that joviality of fifteen minutes ago? She wanted to let rip, really scream at him, but she forced herself not to for her mum's sake.

"Albert..." Her mum's voice. "I really don't think Molly intended to —" It was about time her mum spoke up for her.

"Look, it's outside, all right? And if, during the five minutes since I parked it there, someone has stolen it, I'll save up and buy him another bloody bike!"

And before Albert could lay into her again about her swearing, or worse, before she broke down in front of them all, Molly hurtled from the kitchen and rattled up the stairs to her room. She was so hurt, so determined to get away from them, at that precise moment she *hated* all of them, that she didn't hear the words spoken by her mother as she left: "She's trying her best. Please don't be so harsh with her."

Molly locked her door and flung herself on to her bed.

A bit later her mum came knocking. "Molly?" Molly didn't open the door. She couldn't.

"Come on, Moll, please. Open up." Alice's voice. It wasn't mad. It was soft and concerned.

Molly considered it, but she couldn't. She felt bunched up inside.

Twelve

The bicycle incident of the previous evening was uppermost in Molly's thoughts when she woke at first light. She felt heavy-in-her-stomach-*blue* and longed to escape. While all was still quiet she crept from her room, down the stairs and out of the hotel. After a swim and a mad sprint along the beach she flung herself on to the sand. It was growing windy and the sea was choppy. The wind exhilarated her. It seemed to blow the cobwebs of sadness away. From where she was sitting she could see the ferries ploughing to and from the mainland.

She fantasized about running off, but where could she go? To her dad and Kasia? She'd run from that pain once already. Back to Daniela and her family? In a few weeks Dan would be leaving Poland for France, returning to Trouvai. And if she, Molly, skipped it now all hope of being reinstated at college, of being with her pals at the California again, would fly out of the window. She had to stick this out, make the most of things, find a positive way through. She would dream up ideas for her musical and bury herself in her scribblings, at least until she heard from Madame Savère.

The sand was being blown by the wind in sharp prickly whorls which settled in the folds of her

notebook. It stung her fingers and made it uncomfortable to write. She closed her book and wondered
what to do with herself. She wasn't ready to face her
mum and the others at the hotel yet, so she decided to
take a hike up the rocky beach track to the fortress and
have another go at visiting the dungeons.

She presented herself once more at the fortress gates.
The gatekeeper peered at her from inside his booth. He
was a gruff, toothless old man. "You again!" was his sole
comment.

"Please let me in. I'm writing a musical about the Man
in the Iron Mask. It'll be brilliant and performed all
over France!"

He grunted and squinted at her incredulously.
Nothing she said would persuade him to let her in.

"Come back this evening if you want to see the story
of the Man in the Iron Mask," he conceded eventually.
"There's a pageant taking place on the battlements."

The promise of a pageant lifted Molly's spirits.

"It'll be a gusty old show, I reckon, the way this wind's
carryin' on. We're in for a rough night on the island,
mark my words. Bad storm comin' in."

"But the pageant's definite, is it?"

"Never been cancelled yet. There'll be no more boats
comin' in, though, that's for sure."

"Cheers! Thanks!"

Albert was stripping shutters in the garden when Molly
arrived back at the hotel. Glimpsing him busy at work,
perched near the sheds, she made a swift detour.
Careering around two palm trees she almost tripped
over in her determination not to be spotted by him.

"Molly!"

Shoot!

She slowed down, trying to avoid actually stopping.

"Shout to Philippe to come out, please. I need assistance."

Nodding, she moved off again.

"Molly?"

She swung round, trying not to catch Albert's eye.

"The bike was there, where you left it. So... er, we can forget all that nonsense about you forking out for another one."

"Fine." She walked on. It hurt to stay mad at someone, to harden her heart. She recognized his clumsy peacemaking, but she didn't look back, couldn't smile, preferred to hurt. She consoled herself by arguing silently that she wasn't responsible for the way she felt towards him.

As she passed the kitchen her mother called out to her.

Shoot!

Was she destined to bump into the whole bunch of them when she least wanted it? She peered gingerly around the door and saw that Alice was smiling warmly. "Fancy a glass of lemonade?"

"Thanks." All that swimming and hiking had made Molly thirsty, and there was no denying that her mum made brilliant lemonade even if she was still angry with her.

Alice crossed the scruffy, half-built kitchen with Molly's glass. "I picked the lemons fresh from a tree in the garden this morning. We couldn't do that in Paris, could we?"

Molly tightened with mistrust.

Her mother's expression remained open and smiling. Her eyes were bright and cheerful. Molly tried not to look into them. It made it difficult for her to stay angry.

Her mum was lovely-looking. Not gorgeous like Kasia or Vanessa, but definitely too lovely for Albert.

Molly took a long, thirst-quenching gulp of lemonade. It tasted even better than usual, probably because
she was so in need of a drink. It couldn't be because of
Albert's silly lemon trees! Her mum stroked her on the
forehead. It was a tender gesture.

"Shall we talk, sweetheart?"

"What about?"

"Your future. A new school. There are several on the
mainland. We visited Philippe's yesterday."

Molly sipped at her drink. She considered how best to
respond, how much to give away. "You're staying here
then? That's definite, is it?"

"Well, it's up to you too. We know you're having a
difficult time adjusting. I've explained to Albert that
you're not used to a father—"

"He's *not* my dad and I don't like him."

"He can see that. We both can. You are making it
fairly obvious—"

"Yeah, well…"

"Molly, sweetheart, we both appreciate how much you
love your father. Albert's way is… different. He's
stricter, I realize that – possibly too strict – but he's a
decent and honourable man and he cares for us. Both
of us. What do you say?"

"I wrote to Madame Savère. I've messed things up, I
told her. I've said I'm sorry and I've asked her to give
me another go."

This information took Alice by surprise. She
remained silent, digesting it.

"I don't want to be here, Mum. I want us to live in
Paris, be near Dad… " The force of Molly's resistance
was disquieting.

"Molly—"

"Please listen to me, Mum. If you're really going to
stay here with *him*, then… that's your business. I'll come

and visit, but I don't want to live here. No, wait, please. It's got nothing to do with you and Dad being divorced or me being mad about not knowing. Albert's not my dad, that's all."

"Molly, you ran away from your father and even when he's living in the same city we rarely see him, and you have been expelled. Those are the facts. Now we have to find you another school. Albert is offering us a home here—"

"I think you just want to stay here because you feel insecure and guilty."

"Insec—? Guilty?"

"About being on your own and not providing me with a stable background. All that stuff. Maybe I'm wrong, maybe this is what you want, but it's not for me."

"Not for you? Living with your mother?"

"Please, Mum. If they'll have me I'd like to go back to college. I want to continue with the California. We can have concerts, a cinema there – that's what I enjoy. I'll work really hard to keep my scholarship if they'll give it back to me."

Alice let out a long, slow breath. "Your mind is made up then is it?"

"Yes."

"Would you like me to telephone Madame Savère and have a word?"

"Would you?"

"If you're sure…"

"Positive."

"I'll call after lunch."

"Thanks." Molly kissed her mother on the cheek and mounted the stairs to her room. "I'd better shout for Philippe, or I'll get shot. *Philippe!*"

"Molly…"

"Yeah?"

"About the bicycle. It was ridiculous that Alb— that we all became so upset. I should have—"

"Forget it."

It was the shards of broken glass glinting on the bare floorboards that Molly noticed first. Then, as her gaze travelled about the room she caught sight of the photo frame. Her precious photo frame.

It was lying on the floor at the foot of her bedside table, buckled and twisted. Molly stood frozen at the door before slowly stepping forward into her room. It had contained the photo of her father. She was bemused and shaken. The frame could not have just fallen and smashed into smithereens and scattered itself about the floor of its own volition. It must have been wilfully destroyed.

She slammed the door soundly and stooped to pick up the pieces. Her treasured frame was damaged beyond repair while the photo which had lived within it was so gnarled that her dad's face was now unrecognizable. Why would anyone do such a stinking rotten thing? Who would do it? While asking herself these questions, while fondling the photograph, she caught sight of a sheet of exercise paper on her pillow. In bold black lettering a message on it read:

KEEP AWAY FROM HERE OR YOU WILL DIE.
THE MAN IN THE IRON MASK

Suddenly one of the floorboards behind her creaked. She wasn't alone! In terror, she swung round.

It was Philippe, skulking behind the door.

Without a thought, Molly lunged towards him, screaming "You pig! What did you do that for?" Her face was flushed with rage as she pummelled his chest with her fists.

"Molly!" A voice from beyond the room. Footsteps pounding on the uncarpeted stairs.

"I hate you! I hate everything about this place!"

The door was flung open and Albert burst in.

"Stop this! I said stop!" Albert pulled her away from his son and he pushed her, forced her, dragged her, weeping to the bed.

"Philippe, what in heaven's name is going on here?"

"It was on the ground. I didn't see it... I... was leaving something on her pillow... I... stepped on it..." Philippe was trembling with terror.

Puzzled, Albert looked at the remains of the tattered photo in Molly's hands, the glass on the floor. And before Molly knew what was happening he swung back to his son and belted him hard across the back of the head.

THWACK!

"You had no right to be in here in the first place! Do you hear me?"

The violence of the gesture, its echo in the room, shocked all three of them. In a voice that was barely audible, Albert continued, "Go to your room, son."

Philippe stared at his father with hot, glistening pain, and then fled.

The atmosphere in the hotel throughout the afternoon was grim. Molly stayed in her room, lying on her bed and listening to the wind outside gathering pace just as the old gatekeeper had forecast. It rattled at the shutters, beating them back against the walls. It was awesome. It suited the general mood of things, as though some spirit was out there, forcing its way in, cursing the household, hungry to reap its terrible revenge. Molly couldn't remember when she had last felt so trapped or miserable.

The bedside clock ticked the afternoon away while the

wind outside grew in force. Molly decided against
mentioning the pageant to anyone. She would just go.
Her mother and Albert were decorating one of the
rooms and the sound of a radio playing drifted up to
her. On several occasions during the course of the
afternoon she heard Albert shouting up the stairs to
Philippe to come down but there was no response from
his room across the hotel corridor. At around five,
Molly grabbed her waterproof and slid out the back
door.

Dozens of spectators were assembled on the
battlements. Molly was amazed. She had almost
expected that there would be no one but herself. She
negotiated a path to one of the benches and sat down.
The wind roared around her ears while beyond the
fortress walls the waves slapped against the rocks. The
violence of the weather somehow eased her pain.

And then from out of nowhere, in amongst the late
arrivals, Molly caught sight of her mum and Albert.
They were holding hands. Molly tried not to notice. Her
mum was waving and mouthing something. From such
a distance Molly had no idea what she was saying. In
response she shook her head, meaning *I can't hear you*.

Alice and Albert found themselves places not next to
each other but in the same row. Molly was glad that they
weren't able to sit together. She noticed that she was
chewing her nails. She did that when she thought mean
things about other people.

What did her mum see in Albert?

She could hear her dad's voice repeating the words:
Molly, you have to learn to let go. Did all of this hurt her so
badly because she wasn't letting go? Weren't parents
meant to stay together? To be there, and keep it all in
place for their kids? None of it made any sense. There

was her mum, there was her dad. She loved them both. That was what made sense.

The drums rolled, floodlights dimmed, spotlights blazed. The pageant was commencing.

An actor strode up on to the battlements. He was tall, long-haired and wearing a mask which fitted like a hood over his entire head and his wrists were bound together with rope; here was the heroic prisoner. Enter the Man in the Iron Mask! He paused magnificently for all to see him and then stepped forward to the centre of the stage. A black cloak hung from his shoulders, swirling dramatically as he moved. His iron mask resembled an antiquated space helmet – it was brilliant! Two soldiers with swords followed a few steps behind him.

Molly was imagining the scene set to rock music. Score penned by Jean, Michel and her dad, acoustic guitar played by Dominik.

And then, without any warning, a bell began to clang and went on sounding. The actors gave up on their performances and looked about them. Clearly this wasn't part of the play.

Molly was confused. What was going on? Suddenly she caught sight of Albert. He was forcing his way through the rows of spectators, falling over feet in his haste while Alice looked on after him. Was he ill? Was the bell something to do with him?

The floodlights were switched back on. A blaze of power lit up the general confusion. The bell clanged on incessantly, its beating growing more urgent. The crowd seemed lost, uncertain what to do, until a voice from among them called out, "Look out there! On the water! There's a dinghy smashed against the rocks!"

From one of the fortress towers a spotlight sped in sweeping circles until it lit up the sea and rocks below.

Albert had disappeared down some stone steps. The

two actors who had been playing the soldiers were casting off their costumes and following in the same direction.

Molly's mother came hurrying towards her, shoving her way through the clusters of people. "Molly!" she cried. "Molly, have you seen Philippe?"

Molly shook her head. "What's going on?"

"Philippe's missing… There's a boat out on the water … That was the rescue alarm…"

Molly had no opportunity to reassure her mum that, according to Albert, Philippe was an A1 sailor and it was daft to fear it might be him out there, because before she could utter a word Alice had rushed on.

Molly found her mother on the beach, standing with a crowd in front of the lifeboat. The boat was being made ready for cast-off. Albert, dressed in wellingtons and yellow oilskins, was leading the rescue team which consisted of the two actors and himself.

The weather was so wild now and the curtain of mist so low that it was impossible to see more than a few metres out to sea. The waves were lashing furiously. If there really was a dinghy out there, its chances were slim.

Molly approached her mum, who had stepped forward to the water's edge. Her arms were clasped around her waist as though she was trying to keep warm or prevent herself from shaking. "It couldn't be him, Mum."

"Albert said it is."

"He wouldn't have gone out in this weather. He'd be crazy."

"He was upset. His father hit him. First time he's ever done that."

Molly didn't reply. She felt rotten. If she hadn't made a fuss about the photo this might never have happened.

On the other hand, Philippe shouldn't have done it.

Why was life so complicated?

They stood waiting for hours. Everyone else had drifted off. The sharp wind of an hour earlier had turned to heavy, beating rain. There was nothing to see except the storm, and there was no way of knowing what was happening out there. It was bitterly cold and dark now. The lifeboat had long since vanished from sight.

"I think we should go back to the hotel, Mum." It was the first exchange between them in a while. Alice shook her head.

"But it's freezing standing here."

"You go back then. When Albert comes ashore he'll need my support. I'll wait."

"It's too dark to find anybody."

"That's why I must wait."

"I bet Philippe's tucked up in bed asleep. He'll laugh his head off when he hears about this."

"Molly, *someone's* out there! A boat was sighted, and so was a figure in the water. Philippe's missing. Now, if you don't want to wait then go home, but stop moaning, for heaven's sake!"

Molly was dumbfounded. She hadn't intended to moan. In fact, she hadn't been thinking about herself at all. She'd been concerned about how damp and shivery her mum was looking.

"Forgive me, sweetheart. I didn't mean to snap."

"I'll look in his room. If he's there I'll come and tell you. And I'll stick the kettle on ready for when you and Albert come up." Molly took off her jacket and hung it around her mum's shoulders. "See you later, then." Without waiting for a response, she sprinted off along the beach, clambering up the rocks to the winding lane which led back to the hotel.

There were lights on but Philippe wasn't in his room. Nor was he anywhere else in the hotel. Molly even checked the attic in case he was kidding about, hiding there. Finally, she went down to the kitchen, filled the kettle – sponging up some water she spilt in case Albert moaned about it – and left it on the hotplate to boil.

And then it suddenly occurred to her that someone ought to check if Philippe's dinghy was still tied up along the shore. She ran out into the garden, beating a path through the swaying pine trees, her trainers sinking into the spongy wet sand, until she reached the wooden boathouse. It was empty.

Along the shoreline as far as she could see there was nothing, except broken branches and churning foamy waves. "Philippe!" she screamed, but her voice was immediately swallowed up by the violent wind.

Shoot!

When she got back to the hotel Albert and Alice were sitting opposite each other at the kitchen table. Mugs of tea steamed between them. Her mum's hands were resting on Albert's clasped fists, cupping them. His head was bent.

"Hi," said Molly uncertainly. It felt like an intrusion.

Albert lifted his head. His cheeks were red and weatherbeaten. He stared hard at her. His eyes were blazing and glistening, blinking back tears. He was crying!

Seeing him so vulnerable threw Molly for six and so she was quite unprepared for the ferocity with which he spoke. "Where the hell have you been? Don't you think we've got enough to be anxious about? You never consider anyone except yourself!"

It made her reel. His voice struck her with the same force as the slap which had landed on Philippe that very afternoon.

But what was really unexpected was that she wasn't mad at him. Suddenly she didn't hate him any more. She stood her ground and stared back into his face, seeing him in a different light. This new Albert was a man who was so unhappy that he didn't know how to deal with things.

Molly knew nothing of his past because she had never been interested enough to ask. He had brought Philippe up alone, her mum had told her that much. Now he might have lost him – his only son. If Philippe was dead Albert would have to let go of him.

Look how hard she was finding it to let go of her parents' marriage! Look how tough it was for her not to have her dad there and to watch her mum growing fond of someone else. If she was feeling such pain and confusion, then what must Albert be feeling right now if Philippe had drowned?

Scared. Albert had snapped at her because he was terrified – terrified in case he had lost his only son. He was battling against this fear, resisting the possible truth of it just as Molly had been resisting the loss of her parents' marriage. Coming to terms with things, letting go, was tough for everyone. She wasn't the only one having difficulties.

"I went to the boathouse," she explained slowly. "I went to see if... if Philippe's dinghy was there."

"I checked earlier," Albert replied softly. "There's no sign of it."

She wanted to hold out her hand, to go and comfort him, but she felt afraid – afraid in case he snapped at her again, and afraid to admit how she had misunderstood him. "Albert, Philippe's going to turn up safe. I'm sure he is." Albert looked at her. He needed so badly to believe what she was telling him, at least as much as she wanted to. But the truth was she just didn't know. "Is there anything I can do?" Molly asked.

"I think we should all try and get some rest." It was her mum talking. She was smiling now, full of understanding as though she recognized Molly's confusion, her struggle to express the change that she was experiencing.

Molly nodded. She was about to leave them alone. Then, on impulse, she stepped into the kitchen and kissed her mother and Albert. A clumsy, awkward peck on the top of each head – before hurrying from the room.

Albert's bald pate tasted salty.

Thirteen

Philippe had been washed ashore. He was found in a rock pool by a stranger early next morning.

The wind had dropped and Albert and his fellow sailors were out in the lifeboat. A chopper had been radioed over from the mainland. It was circling the island in search of the boy himself or floating debris from his dinghy. The sound of the rotor beating through the still air was eerie.

Philippe wasn't dead. Several of his ribs were broken from having been smashed against the rocks, one leg was fractured and he was suffering from shock and hypothermia. *But he wasn't dead*! Alice said it was a miracle.

Someone radioed the lifeboat to call Albert back. The chopper landed on the beach, sending out hazy golden sprays of sand. It waited there, like a giant humming insect, for the stretcher bearing Philippe's unconscious body to be stowed safely aboard, ready to whisk him across to the hospital on the mainland.

Molly stood on the beach close to her mum. They watched as Albert accompanied the stretcher, holding Philippe's hand, talking to his son. The boy couldn't possibly hear his father. Albert knew that and so did Molly, but she guessed Albert needed to say certain things.

He was speaking in a really soft voice and weeping.

Not just glistening eyes like the night before, but proper tears rolling down his cheeks. She supposed he was apologizing for clouting Philippe, for being tough with him. Molly was moved by how much Albert loved his son. She admired him for what he was doing. Apologizing took courage.

She had been intending to say sorry for her hostility towards Albert, but she hadn't been able to form the words. It had been too difficult. So she had left it, let the moment pass. She'd kidded herself that Albert was too concerned about Philippe to care what she was feeling, but that was a feeble excuse for not being brave enough.

She wished now that she had spoken up. She could feel proud of herself and it would have pleased her mum. Shoot, she had been making life so difficult, not only for Albert, but for herself and everyone around her. Even if she hadn't meant to. Getting kicked out of college, rowing with her dad, running off, concealing the truth from Dan's Grandad, fighting with Philippe, being belligerent with Albert and misjudging him... And what about her mum? She hadn't considered her mum's feelings at all. The only positive bit was the California. Molly still felt good about that.

The stretcher was finally loaded aboard the helicopter. Albert was on the point of climbing in after it when he stopped and turned. He looked back towards Molly and her mother and approached them.

"I'll call you from the hospital," he said, brushing his hand gently against Alice's cheek. "You take care of your mother for me, eh, Molly?" Molly nodded. And with that he was gone.

Standing with her mum Molly watched the chopper's windswept departure – a bird of rescue rising raucously towards the sky. Once it had disappeared from view they strolled wearily back along the beach to the hotel.

"Tired?" asked Alice.

"Bushed," replied Molly. "What happened to Philippe's mum? Did Albert divorce her?"

"No, she died when Philippe was a baby."

"Didn't Philippe ever know her then?"

"Not really."

How thoughtless she'd been! At least Molly still had both her parents, even if they were no longer together.

Back at the hotel Alice disappeared to telephone Madame Savère. She warned Molly not to wander off; she might be needing her.

Madame Savère had received Molly's letter. She had been delighted to hear of the sum raised by the benefit concert. She had met the two unemployed local boys Molly had chosen as her assistants (*assistants*!) and, yes, she had been informed by both the council and Mr Beauchamps that the California had been awarded a licence to screen films. What was more, she had received a number of letters from parents who had attended the benefit evening. They had written to express their appreciation and delight and to applaud the ingenuity of the youngsters involved.

How reassuring, several had stated, to know that the pupils of Trouvai College were being encouraged to contribute. "It would appear", one mother had written, "that our young are discovering ingenious directions, appropriate to their world, which surely must assist them to carve their futures." Several other letters had applauded Madame Savère on the initiative of such unconventional educational methods. Mr Beauchamps had also written to Madame Savère because he was of the opinion that the California would be a great deal less dynamic without the drive and enthusiasm of Molly Greenfield.

"Well," said Alice, blushing with pride, "I take it Molly will be invited back?"

Madame Savère responded gravely. "Mrs Greenfield, in spite of all that Molly has achieved, she has flaunted the rules of the college and, by doing so, set a disruptive tone. Touched as I am to receive the request from Molly, I am not convinced that taking her back, reinstating her scholarship, is our best course of action."

"For who?" demanded Alice crossly. "For the college or for Molly?"

"Let me have a word with her, please."

Molly was summoned to the living room.

"If this is what you really want, Molly," Alice whispered, "then you must persuade Madame Savère yourself."

With that she handed the receiver over to Molly, who closed her eyes, took a deep breath and said, "Hello."

"Molly, thank you for your letter."

"It was nothing," responded Molly nervously.

"Molly, I would like you to explain to me why you think I should allow you to return here. I am not yet convinced that you could be an asset to the college and not that unruly youngster who pays no heed to the rules of the establishment."

Molly watched her mother smiling encouragingly, while she remained silent. Her mind was a jumble. Her whole future lay in the balance. What could she possibly answer to such a challenge?

"Molly?"

"Yes, I'm here."

"Well?"

"When we lived in England, even when my dad had no work and was blue about it, we were a family. I thought nothing could take that away from me. I felt safe and I resented being sent away. I felt sorry for myself, out of place, not like the others. I *wanted* you to kick me out so I could go home and sort out my folks…" She paused. She was missing her own point.

"I know all that, Molly."

Why was this so difficult? She knew her feelings and what all of this meant to her – all that she had discovered during the preceding year.

"We have to step out there. Folks or no folks. Involve others. Make things happen… bring people together. That's what the California's about. Positive energy… Musicians do it… Phil Collins…"

"Phil Collins!?"

"Phil Collins, Band Aid. Those guys use their music to make others feel good… help people… the starving in Africa, Aids and…"

"Forgive me, Molly, what has this altruism to do with you coming back to school?"

Molly sighed. She had to gather together the kernel of all this rambling, before Madame Savère lost patience with her.

"I tried to make someone on this island feel bad because he cares about my mum, and I didn't want that … but it went wrong… caused an accident."

"Molly, you have caused an accident?!"

"No, please… there was an accident which might never have happened if I hadn't been so selfish… *What am I struggling to say*!!? No self-pity. Your words, Madame."

"My words, yes."

"Good vibes. Yeah, that's it! Find what's positive, not negative. Then life rolls more smoothly."

"Does it, indeed?"

She was making headway. It gave her confidence. "That's why I'm proud of the California… It's why I want to come back to college. It's not the exams and the status and…"

"They are very important, Molly. Particularly in today's world…"

"I'm not ruling them out! But…" she inhaled. Her breathing felt wobbly. "My dad says: Follow your dreams, Moll. And that's all we were doing… even if we shouldn't have gone against you… You… old people get stuck… about rules and stuff. You have to have them, OK, but they can't be all it's about… Us kids… we have to take a fresh look at things, be willing to start all over when life's not working… create what *we* believe in … That's the California. Maybe I went about it the wrong way. I'm sorry… I'm learning about that… *Please* don't kick me out because I handled it badly. The California… it's the beginning of something. That's why I want to come back, please."

She couldn't explain any more, wasn't able. Run out of steam. Probably had said too much already. There was a silence, loud and clear, shouting at her from the other end of the phone.

Shoot! She had gone too far!

"Madam Savère?" No response. She shouldn't have said "you old people", but she'd been lost in her muddled attempt at expressing what all this meant to her. She tried once more. "Madame Savère?" Still no response. The line was dead.

Molly replaced the receiver and stood staring at the telephone while Alice looked on.

"I always manage to rub her up the wrong way."

"She said no?"

"Cut me off."

"You convinced *me*."

Molly didn't reply. What now? she was thinking.

"So I have a daughter who dreams of changing the world?"

"Doesn't everybody?"

"I don't think so."

"Well, none of it means much if I can't even make Madame Savère change her mind."

"Might that statement come under the heading 'Self-pity'?"

Molly lifted her head and looked at her mum. She was laughing silently. Molly relaxed. "You're right."

"You've built the California once, Molly —"

"What's to stop me doing it somewhere else? Never say die, right? Maybe I'll ask the council for permission to use the fortress as a —"

The telephone rang. Molly picked up the receiver.

"I'm not in the habit of being cut off, Molly."

"But I didn't —"

"Now it's my turn. The world out there, my girl, is not as it was when your father was growing up. These revolutionary – dare I say sixties – notions are all very well, but results are what count in this day and age."

"There are heaps of kids out there who've got degrees and still can't find jobs —"

"Let me speak, please." The headmistress's voice was brisk and firm. "You may return to our college —"

"*What?*"

"Listen, please. Your scholarship is reinstated. Not – I repeat *not* – because I am in agreement with much of what you have said, but because you have discovered courage, Molly. Because you have faith in your convictions and you stand by them. Those convictions may change. I hope that Trouvai will play its part in forming your perspective. In the meantime you have won my respect – not an easy task – and you have won the love of many of your fellow pupils, which counts for a great deal. Enjoy the rest of your holiday, Molly. I expect you in September." And the line went dead, the dialling tone buzzing away like a merry bee in Molly's ear because she was too stunned to let go of the phone.

"Brilliant!" she whooped.

Fourteen

Alice was outside the hotel, standing patiently in the lane, drinking in the early September sun. Molly could see her through the window as she leaned over to give Albert and Philippe a farewell hug. It was an amicable parting. She was promising to come back again.

"Whenever you can," said Albert, embracing her tightly. "You'll always be welcome, you and your mum. Make sure she comes back to visit us, eh?"

"But —?"

"She'll explain."

Molly swung her backpack on to her shoulder. "Bye, then!" she called, scooting off after her mum who, by now, had begun to walk on down the hill towards the waiting ferry. She's getting anxious, thought Molly.

"Got everything?" Alice asked with a smile when Molly caught up with her.

"Yeah."

They walked along in silence for a moment or two.

"Mum, what did Albert mean when he said *we'd* always be welcome here? He said you'd explain."

"I'm going back to Paris."

Molly stopped dead and turned to face her mother. "You're not staying with him?"

Alice shook her head. She was squinting from the

glare in the sunlight. "I've been looking in the papers for a job."

"I thought you wanted to stop here with Albert, that you were planning on marrying him."

"No." Alice stepped on a pace or two. She was conscious of the ferry departure and Molly's connecting train.

Molly stayed put, looking after her mum. "What made you change your mind?"

"You."

"*Me*?" Now she hurried to catch up, to read the expression on her mother's face. "In what way, me?"

"Your faith."

"I don't understand."

"I think you were right, my darling. I did bring us here to Albert's because I feared the alternative – bringing you up alone, facing life in a new city, a new country... without your father."

"If that's what's troubling you we could go back to England."

"No, your school is here, and anyway it wouldn't change anything."

"Why not?"

"I still have to face what lies ahead – finding work, beginning again. Even in England."

"Maybe you and Dad will get back together again. We'll all be in Paris like we always dreamed."

"Don't hope for that, Molly."

"Nothing's impossible."

"No, nothing's impossible, Molly. But dreams don't always turn out the way we plan them."

"Sometimes they turn out better."

Alice burst out laughing.

"No, seriously, Mum! Look at me and college and all the great stuff that's happening at the California."

They had reached the landing stage. The scent of algae drifting from the warm sea washed over them.

Alice brushed a hand across her daughter's shoulder and drew her close. "Such an optimist you are, Molly. Your father's daughter. And that optimism is a part of your magic. It's precious, my darling. Don't lose it."

Molly grinned. She turned as they arrived at the gangplank. "Mum, I want to say... sorry. Sorry. You know, for hurting you and for being a pain."

Alice smiled. She was touched by her daughter's words.

"Are you going to be all right, Mum?"

"Of course, silly girl! But thank you for asking."

"Don't cry, please, Mum."

"Got your tickets?"

"You've asked me twice already!"

"I know. Oh, Molly, I promised myself I wouldn't cry. Come here and give me a hug."

Molly slung her backpack to the ground and threw her arms around her mother. She smelt good – minty, flowery. "I love you," she whispered and gathered up her bag. Seconds later, she was on the boat.

Alice watched from the shore as Molly negotiated her way through a gaggle of parting tourists. She dropped her bag to the ground and stepped forward, swinging like a monkey on the railing.

"See you in Paris for Christmas!" Her straw hair shone like golden wheat stalks in the morning sunshine. "Or maybe Gdansk!" She was beaming from ear to ear.

The boat began to move, slipping slowly away from the quay. Molly waved furiously.

"Careful you don't fall!" Alice called back, glimpsing for the first time the young teenager emerging in front of her. Her heart soared with pride.

"Bye, darling!" she cried, to the wild, bright girl with

dreams and hopes as big as the world.

Molly!

She wished her every one of those dreams.